W9-BYP-666

The Hound of Heaven at My Heels

ROBERT WALDRON

The Hound of Heaven
at My Heels

The Lost Diary of Francis Thompson

IGNATIUS PRESS   SAN FRANCISCO

DEDICATED TO
PATRICK BROWN, O.C.S.O.
MONK OF SAINT JOSEPH'S ABBEY
SPENCER, MASSACHUSETTS

Acknowledgment

Sincere thanks to Mr. Joseph Tedeschi, alumnus of Boston College, whose kindness and generosity opened to me the doors of the Boston College Library, in which is housed the largest collection of Thompson papers.

Prologue

I first learned of Francis Thompson's diary from a letter of Reverend Terence L. Connolly, S.J., of Boston College, to Mr. Wilfrid Meynell, editor of the Catholic monthly *Merry England*. Mr. Meynell had passed on most of Thompson's papers to Reverend Connolly, who was at the time the foremost Thompson scholar in America. It is sad to note, however, that he likely followed Wilfrid Meynell's mandate that anything "unfit" about Thompson was to be burned.

In the late 1980s I was in search of books for my work on the great Victorian poet, deciding that his present obscurity needed to be addressed, for I have no doubt that Thompson is one of England's great poets. My book dealer, Mr. Gloss, ransacked his collection but found nothing that I didn't already own. The one volume I desperately needed for my research was Father Connolly's *Francis Thompson and His Paths*, subtitled *A Visit to Persons and Places Associated with the Poet*. Mr. Gloss admitted that he had in storage many more books and said that he'd look them over, but it was unlikely, he warned me, that he'd find such an obscure book.

A month later I received an elated call from Mr. Gloss informing me not only that he had found the book but also that he had in hand a nice surprise for me. I rushed to his shop in Boston. With his face smiling beatifically, he handed me Connolly's book; it was in mint condition. "Open it", Mr. Gloss urged. The book opened to pages between which lay a folded paper, a letter from Reverend Terence Connolly to Wilfrid Meynell. Unfolding the tissue-thin, yellowish paper, I read Father Connolly's confession to burning everything he considered "unnecessary" about Francis Thompson. I sighed as I read this, knowing how Thompson scholars would forever be disappointed. But then my heart raced as I read the letter's last paragraph:

> My dear Wilfrid, you were indeed correct about our poet's diary, because it does exist. A barely decipherable entry in one of his dilapidated notebooks indicates that he kept a diary during his stay at Storrington 1889–1890. He sequestered it in his cell under a floor plank. You must journey to the monastery to seek it. Who knows what it contains.
>
> > In Christ,
> > Terence L. Connolly, S.J.

I would have paid Mr. Gloss a fortune for both the book and the letter, but, knowing my passion for Thompson, he charged me only a modest sum, for which I will always be grateful. I am sure he could have placed the letter on the auction table and received much more for this precious Thompsoniana. He kindly warned me not to get my hopes up about finding the diary.

"It's been a hundred years", he said, shaking his head. "It's unlikely you'll find the diary."

"If I do find it, I shall publish it. But I'll hand over the proceeds to Boston College."

"What about the letter?"

"It will become a part of the BC collection."

He nodded his head in approval; we shook hands, and I left his bookstore with both Connolly's book and letter.

I wondered why the letter had never been sent only later to discover that it had been written a few days before Father Connolly's death. The next puzzle was how the book had ended up in Mr. Gloss' bookshop. It seems that Mr. Gloss' father had an understanding with all the local Jesuits: when priests died, the elder Mr. Gloss was the first to be summoned over the dispersing of libraries. Although Jesuits take vows of poverty, during their lives they often accumulate fine libraries, as many of them are professors and scholars and teach at the several Jesuit colleges in the Boston area.

I immediately booked my trip to England in hopes of retrieving the diary. I made London my base, and the day after my arrival I set out by car to Storrington in Sussex.

I rather love the English countryside, which possesses a voluptuous green foreign to New England. Perhaps its richness is due to the clouds and rain, but I was in no mood to savor Marvel's green, my thoughts returning over and over to the lost diary. My greatest fear was that it had been discovered and removed and would never be found. Perhaps a Storrington monk had come upon it and returned it to the poet himself. Perhaps the religious order itself had sequestered the diary in its scriptorium.

Thompson had always intended to write a diary in imitation of De Quincey's famous *Confessions of an Opium-Eater.* I dreamed that Thompson's diary would be the equal of De Quincey's masterpiece, taking the literary world by storm. Then once and for all Thompson's genius would be recognized.

Finally, after driving down a long, winding road bordered by great yew trees, I arrived at the Priory of Our Lady of England, established by the Canons of Prémontré in the midnineteenth century. When I rang the bell, a loud gong echoed through the priory. I waited for ten minutes before venturing to search for one of the monks. I walked through a corridor that led into the sun-splattered cloister. In the middle of the garth stood a statue of Mary of England.

"May I help you?" asked a cultured voice behind me.

I turned to find a kindly looking young man in a white habit. His gentle eyes seemed amused to see me. So eager was I to begin my search for the diary, I had unconsciously invaded the privacy of the cloister—no small violation.

"Are you lost?"

"I'm sorry, but I waited for ten minutes at your door. I'm Robert Waldron."

"Ah, the Thompson scholar", he said, reaching out to shake my hand while he introduced himself as Brother Luke, the retreat master. "You're to stay with us for a few days and wish to reside in Thompson's former room? Yes, fine, follow me."

I followed him down winding, lowly lit corridors, passing through several doors and entering into an arched cloister leading to the main residence. Along the way, I caught glimpses of the retreatants' refectory, with its two rectangular wooden tables already set for dinner, the library, and the retreatants' chapel—all empty and silent.

We then passed into the dark church by a side door at the end of the east cloister. The church's immense silence and shadow enveloped me, while odors of guttered candles, incense, damp stone, wet wool, and floor polish rushed upon me and brought back memories of the countless hours I'd spent as an acolyte in my own parish church and later during my years in the seminary.

Finally we reached a narrow stairway, up which we climbed. We stood before a small cell, the door ajar.

"This was the great poet's room. As you see, it has a nice view and receives sunlight all during the afternoon. I hope you find it comfortable."

The room was austere, with a bed, chair, desk, and white-washed walls. Above the bed hung a crucifix, rather ancient, judging by the yellow of its ivory corpus. The view of the hills and sky indeed was panoramic. I turned to Brother Luke and thanked him for his kindness; he pointed to the desk, on which lay the schedule for meals and the Liturgy of the Hours. He offered to lead me on a tour of the monastery after dinner.

When I was alone, my first impulse was to look for the diary. But I allowed my hopes to linger a bit longer. I sat on the bed. It was as hard as stone, which pleased me, because I have a weak back and cannot abide too soft a bed. My eyes began to search the floor. Plain oak boards highly waxed. The sunlight streaming through the window transformed them into long slabs of butter. My eyes darted everywhere for a secret hiding place. The boards had lain faithfully side by side for over a hundred years. No gaps, no holes, no irregular or overlapping boards. Neatly and austerely arranged, the kind of fine carpentry I'd expect of monks.

I explored every inch of the floor until I realized I'd forgotten to look under the bed. I dragged the bed to the opposite side of the room. Again everything appeared normal. I got down on my hands and knees and perused each board. All was as tight as a drum. No sign of a secret hiding place.

Later, after lunch, I asked Brother Luke if any work had been done on the priory or if it was as Francis Thompson would remember it. He assured me that nothing had been done to the monastery except that it now had central heating. I sped back to my room and searched beneath the radiator—but found nothing. While on my knees I happened to look into the corner of the room where the bed stood. The last wooden plank didn't quite reach the wall, leaving a small gap. Surely it was wide enough to secrete a diary. I pushed the bed aside, sank to my knees, and stuck my fingers into the gaping space. I felt nothing. With some wiggling of my fingers I was able to thrust my whole hand and wrist inside until I felt what at first I took to be another wooden plank. But it was too smooth to my touch to be wood. My fingers explored the unknown object until I realized my hand had surely grasped a book, which I carefully and slowly extricated. I found in my hand a small leather-bound volume. I blew off the years of accumulated dust before my trembling fingers opened to the first page, where I read:

Dear Francis,
Capture your time at Storrington in this beautiful diary, a gift from your dear friends,

Alice and Wilfrid Meynell

A part of me wanted to exclaim my discovery to the world, but I was not ready to share it with anyone. At dinner Brother Luke saw that I was animated. As he poured coffee into my cup, he looked at me with raised eyebrows.

"If I were superstitious, I'd say you'd met the ghost of Francis Thompson."

"Well, in a way I have."

"How so?"

"Just being in the room where he lived for over a year, I feel closer to him."

"Yes, I can understand that. But you look too pleased about something."

"May I ask if the crucifix on the wall is the same one that hung there in Thompson's time?"

"Yes, nothing changes in monasteries."

"Except the heating system."

He laughed, and I sipped my coffee, trying to appear nonchalant.

There was no reason to stay, and I intended to slip out unnoticed in the night. But my scruples about leaving without informing anyone at the monastery of my find won out. I asked Brother Luke for an interview with the abbot. After Vespers he led me to the abbot's office. A tall man with a kind face, he received me warmly, and I felt quite at ease telling him why I had come to his monastery. When I told him about my discovery of Thompson's diary, he was almost as pleased as I.

"The legend of Thompson's diary has lingered in the air here ever since his biographer came here forty years ago. We searched for it to no avail here and at our motherhouse in France."

"I'll want to publish it, if there is no objection."

"I believe that Thompson hid it knowing someone would eventually discover it and that it would be up to that person to do the right thing. You will not use it for personal gain?"

"No, only to reactivate interest in Thompson's life and his poem *The Hound of Heaven*. The actual diary will become part of the Thompson Collection at Boston College."

"Then go with God."

Shortly after my return to Boston I received confirmation that my book on Thompson's *The Hound of Heaven* had been accepted for publication. I was delighted, for I'd had a difficult time finding a publisher for Catholicism's greatest poet. The house's editor-in-chief, however, was very much aware of the importance of Thompson's verse, and she was dedicated to making the poet better known and appreciated.

I decided not to reveal to anyone else my discovery of the diary until my own book had been published and appreciated. Allow the general public to become reacquainted with Thompson and then reveal the diary. Now that my book has been available for over a year, I am releasing the diary to the world.

Are there any soul-shattering revelations? Well, that depends. In our modern world, which has become more and more voyeuristic, there is probably little here that would raise an eyebrow. But for those with the eyes to see, Thompson's diary will throw much light on the creative process and upon the unyielding power of drug addiction.

An additional value of this diary is that it illustrates how poignantly human Thompson was. Wilfrid Meynell and Reverend Terence Connolly meant well when in their own minds they canonized Francis Thompson. But most of us are not saints, and we need before us role models who are like us, who struggle every day to remain faithful to Christ, a struggle that never ceases.

Thompson is an inspiration to everyone who has been plagued by failure, self-loathing, and/or addiction. He is also an inspiration to everyone who is lonely and feels unloved. May the downcast who read this diary take heart: the man who wrote it lived to the full even when for many years he had only life's lees to drink. But as the poet Jeffers reminds us, "Even in the lees may lie new discovery."

An immense Host in the firmament. A good omen. When we had passed a pond luminous in moonlight, Wilfrid said, "We are almost there."

"Almost." Is there a more forlorn word in the coinage of our language? My almost life, my almost love, my almost ruination, my almost fame. Almost a priest, almost a doctor, almost a poet. Am I not able to wax eloquent about almost?—but—and there is always a but—I failed. The simple truth. Because I failed again, I have come here to this priory, to this monk's cell. How appropriate that I, stripped of everything, should be present here in this cell with bed, desk and lamp, and the holy crucifix on the wall. Life's bare essentials.

Oh, my dear Jesus, I have failed you so dismally! You rescued me through the kindness and compassion of Wilfrid and Alice. You led me from the horror of the loathsome London streets into the light and the warmth and the love of the Meynells' home.

And I tossed all away!

We arrived late and rang the bell innumerable times. Then Wilfrid banged on the door. Finally, a white-hooded monk answered. I could not see his face until moonlight revealed his glittering eyes. If I had been alone, I would have spewed forth my life to this ancient ascetic, whose gaze caused me to tremble.

"I am Wilfrid Meynell, and this is my dear friend Francis Thompson. You are expecting us."

17

"We expected you before sundown", the monk said curtly. We had, I gathered, awakened him.

"Yes, we were unexpectedly delayed, and we are indeed most contrite for any inconvenience we may have caused you."

The monk smiled. Relief spread swiftly throughout my body. Oh, he *is* kind. I must reside only with the kind. Oh, dear God, let me never again abide with the unkind and permit me never to be unkind to any soul.

He led us down a labyrinth of corridors, our only illumination the candle in his bony hand, rendering light and shadow along our seemingly interminable journey. We stopped at Wilfrid's room on the first floor. He turned to me and said, "Go, Francis, the good brother will lead you to your room." He perceived the terror in my eyes. "Francis, I shall pray for you during the night. If you cannot sleep, think of me, for I too shall be awake."

Oh, how he knows me, knows my anxieties, my terrors, and my hauntings. Ever so kind, ever so compassionate. Such love to sacrifice sleep for a friend. My dear Jesus, if only Wilfrid had been with you in Gethsemane.

I cannot sleep. I sit in this cell. It is silent, clean, and safe. Outside are the hills and downs with which I shall soon become acquainted. I yearn for clean air and nature's beauty . . . and silence and solitude. If there are books, I shall endure. And I have, yes, I have in possession—I must admit it here, although it sunders my heart to confess—a small quantity of opium.

I bring it for pain, but I shall not use it. I shall not! How many times have I uttered such a vow? But how could I come to this solitary place so far from London without an analgesic? My teeth ache constantly, my gout is permanent, my cough a stabbing knife, my stomach a caldron of acid. I must have surcease and shall use it only as a last resort. Such a comfort to know it lies quietly in the desk drawer.

It pains me to lie to Wilfrid, but did he not by a look betray his knowledge? Does he not see into the very depths of my soul, and does he not always forgive me?

Not so with Alice. Oh, my dear Alice, what a disappointment I have been to you! You, whom I love not less than Wilfrid; you, the most beautiful woman I have ever known. You, a mistress of poetry. But to you there are limits, as there should be. You judged me, and I was found wanting. Your children indeed must be protected. As if I'd ever harm a hair of their heads! Their shorn curls I should swiftly gather to preserve in a golden reliquary, for they are God's precious ones.

In your compassion you sent me not back to the inferno of the streets but here to purgatory. When I am purged, I shall return to you—if you will permit me again into your presence.

Never to see you or the children, that indeed would be hell.

I cannot sleep. My life arises before me in horror. Must I relive everything again and again? The horror of the Thames embankment, where I slept on the wet ground near the rejected women of the night. Huddled under the bridge arches during torrential rains. Oh, the filthy fumes of the Thames!

The day I awakened before sunrise with the ebony river beckoning to me. How close I came to hurling myself into its darkness, like poor young Emily, who drowned herself after finding she was with child.

But Jesus appeared to me, and I knelt in thralldom until the sun arose, irradiating me with the will to live another day.

Wilfrid is downstairs, where he prays for me. Dear Jesus, hear the prayers of a holy man who believes I shall become a great poet. Dear Jesus, assist me in my silence, assist me in my verse making, and render me worthy of Wilfrid's belief in me.

The bell of Lauds sounded. Then utter silence. No birdcall from the naked trees outside my window. Silence. Then the knock at my door. Brother Placid beckons me to follow him to the chapel for Mass. No time to wash or to shave. My habiliments are shabby, but no one in the cloister takes notice. Or, rather, no one violates custody of the eyes.

I kneel in a stall next to Wilfrid, who looks fresh and alert. He reaches out to pat my hand. His kind, bearded face assures me that all shall be well. The chapel is beautiful in candlelight. The monks arrive singly and slowly. In their white cowled habits they appear like a flock of white birds descending upon a craved feeding ground. The tabernacle is golden and draped in purple. Above the main altar is a huge stained-glass window of the Resurrected Christ.

Returning to myself at the Eucharist, I see the morning sun blaze through the window of Jesus. Light transforms it into an icon of translucent ruby, emerald, and sapphire. Once darkened glass now afire with radiance.

I say, "Domine non sum dignus", because I am ever so unworthy to receive Christ. No, I cannot receive my Lord. Not yet. With folded hands, like a young acolyte, Wilfrid receives Jesus; with eyes cast down, he reverently returns to his stall, where he remains rapt in contemplation.

Oh, how I envy his innocence! He cannot ever imagine

what horrors I have seen, what blasphemies I have heard, to what depths I have descended.

Breakfast in the refectory. Several oaken tables shining in lamplight. Wilfrid and I sit opposite each other. Our simple meal is tea and bread.

"Did you sleep, my dear Francis?"

"No. But I never sleep in a new place."

"I prayed for you to our Blessed Mother."

I could have wept. In all the world is there such a man?

"I could not pray, for my life haunts me."

"You must let it go, Francis. Cast yourself in our Lord's arms. He will take upon Himself all your sins, all your anxieties and fears. He loves you."

My hands tremble. I can barely bring the cup to my lips. Wilfrid's hand reaches out to steady mine, and I quaff luke-warm tea.

I tremble not for opium but because in a short time my dearest friend departs for London. Shall I ever behold him again? Ten years of opium have reduced my body to a mud hut. Will my body heal? And what remains of my intellect? My prose impresses many, but am I capable of poetry? Wilfrid believes I am. But he says I need an ordered existence. Thus I am here. Order: the very thing I have fled all my life.

A day cloudy, and the hills shrouded in mist. The carriage arrives. I stand speechless before my friend. I know not what to do or to say. Wilfrid embraces me for a long time. He holds me at arm's length and looks into my eyes. "You can do it, Francis. I shall daily pray for you . . . you can do it." His eyes are moist. He abruptly releases me and turns to climb into the coach, which sets off immediately. He leans out to wave. I raise my hand to him.

Now begins the beginning—or the end.

The Priory's welcome sheet for guests gladdens my heart. It reads, "Father Abbot and the community are happy to welcome you to our monastery. We sincerely hope that you will find here a place of peace and love in Christ." Then the excerpt from Matthew (11:28–30): "Come unto me, all ye that labor and are heavy laden, and I will give you rest."

The day for guests begins with Lauds and Mass at 6:00 A.M. After Mass a breakfast in silence is followed by Tierce and then Sext. Luncheon at 1:00 is followed by None at 3:00 and Vespers at 6:00; supper at 6:45 and Compline at 8:00 and to bed in silence at 9:00.

I have vowed to Jesus to follow exactly the Liturgy of the Hours. Time sanctified is time transcended, and only in such time shall I vanquish my life's enslavement.

Brother Placid informed me that Abbot Raines wished to meet me and officially welcome me to Storrington. I knew next to nothing about the Abbot except that Wilfrid and he were friends and had attended university together.

"He'll announce your name when he's ready to meet with you. Just sit here until then", Brother Placid said, pointing to the straight-back chair outside the Abbot's office. "Don't be anxious", he whispered. "When Reverend Father keeps people waiting, he's testing their patience—and humility."

I waited for over an hour. Gazing out the cloister window, I watched the cloudscapes race across the sky. Then I heard his cultured voice, "Come in, Francis Thompson."

On entering the room I expected to find a large man, for

his voice was deep and commanding. But I met a diminutive monk, completely bald, half-glasses resting precariously upon the narrow bridge of his nose, over which he stared at me. With ruddy cheeks and a kind face, he could have stepped out of the pages of Charles Dickens. The man tingled with life, and I sensed an aura of holiness about him.

His office was the size of a monk's cell, with a desk and two straight-back chairs. On the stark whitewashed wall hung a crucifix and an icon of Mary and Child. The uncurtained, sparkling window offered a view of the hills, muted in winter hues. The austerity of it all prompted me to simplify my life, to reduce it to zero.

After I knelt and kissed his ring, he said, "Sit down, Francis Thompson. You look tired. Have you eaten?" He gestured toward the chair before his desk.

"Yes, Reverend Father, thank you."

"You've been ill?" he asked gently.

"Yes", I replied.

"You're here to regain your health?"

"That is my hope."

"Your benefactor, Mr. Meynell, said you have been forlorn of late."

"Yes, Reverend Father, if by that you mean unhappy with my life. I have failed at everything."

"Fear not", he said, with a wave of his bony hand. "You are young, with much time to prove yourself. Tell me about your life."

"There's not much to tell. I have been enslaved to opium", I said, ashamed. "My craving nearly killed me."

"Why come here?" he asked, his gaze roving my face.

My own poverty washed over me. Finally I said, "To pray to God to help me."

"So you're here to save yourself?" he asked, his eyes fixed on me.

"I can't do anything but pray", I said, looking him in the eye, as my father had taught me. It was difficult, for I felt he could see into the deepest recesses of my soul—and had seen my emptiness.

"I pray daily for courage," I said, "but I've always known I'm a coward—it's my cross."

He abruptly stood and stepped to the window and looked out toward the hills. He was no taller than five feet. He was completely still, seemingly transfixed by the distant hills. With my heart pounding and my palms sweating, I feared he would surely chastise me or ask me to depart.

When I thought he'd forgotten about me, he quickly turned around. "You are welcome to stay as long as you wish. I have known your benefactor for many years. He says that you are touched with genius and that he hopes it will flower here at our monastery." He sat down and again folded his hands. "I hope you can live our life. But I warn you, our life isn't an escape. Here you'll find a reality you've never dreamed of. I believe, however, that you may indeed receive here the cure you desire. You are committed to a cure, are you not?"

"Yes, I'm committed", I said firmly.

"We shall see."

I stood and thanked him for his kindness. I was at the door when he said, "By the way, you're not a coward."

"I feel like one."

"If you were a coward, you would not be here."

My heart leapt with joy. "Thank you, Reverend Father."

"Before you depart, I must ask you to meet with our Father Sebastian. He is to be your guide while you are living here. I believe you two shall get along quite well. Does that present any problem to you?"

"No, Reverend Father. I'm glad to have someone with whom to speak. Thank you."

"Go with God, Francis."

At last I have found a confessor who completely understands me. Father Sebastian is old and wise, and he knows the world. A monk for forty years, he formerly lived among the world for forty years. He understands the insidious, ensnaring tentacles of opium. He too read De Quincey as a young man and wandered the streets of Charing Cross in a haze, sacrificing all for the "assuaging balm of eloquent opium".

Oh, how fortunate I am to have found such a monk! No, Wilfrid's prayers sent me to this holy monk. Father Sebastian has urged me to make a general confession. I agreed.

"When?" he asked.

"I am not ready", I said, ashamed. He nodded and said, "Readiness is all." To be absolved, to be again a luminous soul, to receive again Christ in the Eucharist—to be reunited with Jesus, my tremendous lover.

Oh, how I long for Jesus! Oh, how I long to be one with Him!

De Quincey's *Confessions of an Opium-Eater.* If I had never opened that Pandora's box! A gift from the loving hands of my dear, departed mother! She had no inkling what magical curse it would exert on a dreamy eighteen-year-old. I devoured it in a few hours; forever it is a part of my very being. I hoped for the visitation of pain or illness to necessitate my use of the drug of Tartarus.

I did not have long to wait. Constant drinking of tea suffused with sugar had eroded my back teeth. A simple toothache (is pain ever simple?) sent me to the chemist in Manchester, where outside the shop I lingered for hours mustering the courage to purchase the needed anodyne. A modicum of opium dismissed my body's aches but also dispatched an unprepared for apocalypse: manifold castles and cathedrals and cloisters descending from shimmering clouds; iridescent oceans upon oceans and lakes upon lakes shining like diamonds and rubies and sapphires! Skyey pavillions of lapis lazuli stretching toward the mountains in endless vistas drenched in golden sunlight. All proclaimed that God's in His heaven and all is right with the world.

Fraught from youth with fear, I became tranquil as a sultan, nodding affirmatively to all processions and visitations.

I was happy.

March 1

I am so hastily taken hither that I am insufficiently prepared for my stay. I have written to Wilfrid. I need boots, my present ones being worn through. My socks are beyond repair. I also need a razor. Of course, I need not shave, but I am wary to grow a beard, for I may frighten the environs' rustics. But above all things I must have books. I begged Wilfrid to send me books. Shakespeare alone would be a blessing and Shelley a dear kindness. Of all the poets I know Shelley best; he is the brother I dreamed to have had. I loved dearly my sisters, but they were not poetical. I remember their lament "up in the moon again", when I was ravished in reverie.

My nerves begin to quiet, but my hands still flutter like fledglings. Sleep has yet to visit me for any time's length. Ah, sleep. Macbeth's dreams murdered sleep. So with me, and I murdered no one. My greatest sin was not the cruel word or deed—it was my silence. Shall I ever be courageous enough to confess to Father Sebastian?

The unutterable sights of London! The bloated baby floating in the murky Thames, the woman's throat slashed from ear to ear, so deeply she was nearly decapitated. The pile of rags in an alley corner that suddenly moved and from which gleamed a green eye. The rats along the Thames and under the bridges' arches— rats outnumbering London's inhabitants.

My surcease of such sights was opium—until the horrors arrived.

March 2

A terrible night. I turned in my bed to behold a rat with green eyes lying upon my desk, observing me. It moved not until I stirred, at which movement it flung itself at me, gnawing at my throat.

I awoke in a panic. Opium beckoned to me from the desk. I fell to my knees and prayed to my tender Mother Mary.

At dawn I awakened on the floor in my nightshirt. Too weary, I missed Lauds but dressed in time for Mass.

Today Father Sebastian and I walked two miles. He is a hale octogenarian. I told him about my beloved Anne, who found me shivering in the arches of Covent Garden. I prayed the policeman would not discover me with his flashing lanterns and expel me again into the icy rain.

But I was detected. "Ere you, get outa that!" he shouted. Like an apparition of Mother Mary, Anne emerged from the London mist (is there a mist more foul in all England?) and raised me up in her arms to lead me to her poor lodgings, where she nursed me back to health.

I confessed to Father my love for Anne. I asked him to pray for her, for I know not whether she is dead or alive. If she is dead, I am certain she is saved, for she fed the hungry, nursed the sick, clothed the naked. Because she loved much, much will be forgiven. She shared her last crumbs with me, her scant pittance. Oh, Anne! Your kind smile, your sad eyes, capable of love after what you had beheld, your voice, ever low and soothing.

My Anne who said, "The first time I saw you I knew you were a genius."

"How?" I asked, amused.

"Your fine brow and eyes proclaim it", she said.

Father asked me if I had sinned with Anne. How is it possible to sin with an angel? Our love was as pure as the lilies of the field. No, she and I never sinned. We slept together in the same bed, chaste as brother and sister. Together we dreamed—yes, we dreamed of marriage, of children, but alas, she disappeared into the London mist to permit my pursuit of poetry. A greater love no woman possesses than to . . .

March 5

The foul rodent haunted me again. Its green eyes watched my every movement. It spoke to me.

"It is here in the desk. Come and take it."

"No."

"It is here in the desk. Come and take it."

"Never."

"You have said such before."

It disappeared. Trembling and perspiring, I lit my candle and sat for hours in prayer. "Dear God, please give me the courage not to succumb", I repeated over and over until my candle guttered and the first light appeared.

My first ingestion of opium was an act of full consent of the will. I was cognizant of the dangers of lifetime enslavement, but I hoped the visionary splendor would nourish my poetic power, and this was of greatest importance to me.

Thereafter my opium drinking was no longer a complete act of the will, for my body developed its own will counter to that of my mind and soul. Oh, how I understand Saint Paul's lamentation, "for the good that I would I do not, but the evil that I would not I do."

Saint Francis named his body Brother Ass. My own body has been more like a faithful canine, faithful to one master: opium. I am plagued by the axiom that an old dog cannot be taught new tricks . . .

March 6

Through the meadow ways I treaded down to the river's edge. The water was still, mirroring the late winter sky. I watched the swans glissade over its sun-splattered surface. No wind. Only silence. I knew then and there that I must learn to know this silence, to become its friend, to render it a part of my being—therein lay Pax.

I remained until the sun commenced its decline, looking like a flame-sopped flower of crimson glory. How faithful is the sun, a daily but sore reminder of my own unfaithfulness.

March 13

A week has passed. I am improved and able to eat. My stomach ailments remain constant, as they have ever since I was a child. Acid stomach, Mother used to say. The result of fear. Always too much fear.

The Priory is situated in a beautiful locus of rolling hills and valley. I have learned that the Cannons Regular of Prémontré, also known as Norbertines, founded this monastery when they were expelled from France during religious persecution. It is now a place of directed retreats or simply rest and relaxation for both spirit and body. Here the racing cloudscapes enthrall me, and the crisp and clear air cleanses my lungs. Yes, Wilfrid and Alice have chosen well in sending me to this place of peace.

Today I met the local shepherd, a reticent man like myself, but we communicated in our silence. He fulfills his vocation happily, although it is not an easy one. "Sheep are stupid animals, but I love them." Christ himself could say the same about us. As if he had read my mind, he laughed. "You need a sense of humor to be a good shepherd."

   "A sense of humor is a virtue to any vocation", I said. He nodded and smiled. I have a friend.

March 20

Bad night. Tumultuous dreams. "Full of scorpions is my mind." Finally I sat up and lit my candle. Jesus gazed down on me from the wall. My books arrived today. Shakespeare, Shelley, and my Bible—their presence a consolation. What more do I need?

Father Sebastian had asked me if I had ever despaired. He knew the answer from my silence. "Had you ever attempted to take your life?" he asked quietly, his old eyes kindly gazing into mine. I wept. Such convulsions of grief I cannot remember. Even in those dark nights in Green Park when I would crawl into the shrubbery for shelter, even when I was so utterly alone, I never wept as I wept today.

   I told him I had once not eaten in five days, having spent my all on opium. Naked beneath my coat, my socks and pants windowed, my stomach gnawed as if by rats, I decided

I had suffered enough. With a lethal quantity of laudanum I went to the back of Covent Garden, where the market rubbish is piled high into pyramids. Amongst the rubbish. Yes, an appropriate place, I felt, to end my life.

I had already drunk half the bottle when the dead boy poet Chatterton encircled my wrist. "No!" he exclaimed. I remembered his suicide and the money he had awaited arriving by post the day after his death. On that scant hope I refrained from imbibing the rest.

Then my poem *The Passion of Mary* miraculously appeared in Wilfrid's *Merry England*, and my life changed forever. My everlasting thanks to Jesus for sending to me the young Chatterton, followed by my dear Wilfrid.

I could not say with certainty to Father Sebastian that I would have finished the deadly dosage. I am too like Hamlet, and too afraid of the eternal fires of hell to commit suicide, but I am yet guilty of mortal sin, for having once made the decision to end my life.

But my greatest sin—shall I be able to confess it and to withstand Father's gaze?

March 21

Sussex and I have become fast friends. The landscape is one of austere undulations of chalk and tundra broken by windswept trees and gorse. Always is my attention riveted to some beauty of land and sky.

Shortly after noon I was swiftly enveloped by mist and could not see the hand before me. Terror rooted me to the spot. Time crawled by. I peered into the mist looking for some opening, some light that would lead me toward safety. But there was nothing but opacity. Finally I sat upon the ground and kept repeating to myself Christ's gentle command, "Be ye not anxious." When the mist dissipated, how appropriate to behold before me a lamb, hugging as I the ground.

Fear and flight were my past life. Waiting is my present one.

Today the sun appeared in my room at noon. I sat in its radiance for the remainder of the afternoon. Images are beginning to arise in my mind again, and poetry is on the horizon.

The Liturgical Hours here are sublime. I have kept my vow to attend them all. Gregorian chant transports me to another world. Glorious simplicity; it is the music of angels, disembodied and as pure as the air of the Storrington Downs.

King Lear—oh, how I understand your blindness, your selfishness and stubbornness. Before you stood Cordelia, the daughter who sincerely loved you, whom you rejected and banished.

My own dear father, whom I love. I am not an Edmund or a Goneril or a Regan, who for worldly gain, filial piety did feign. Truly, I loved my father, but I could not pretend to be the son he wished me to be. I could not be a priest, for I loved too much the world's beauty. I could not be a doctor, because before bloody flesh I fainted. I was what I am—a poet. I should have told him the truth. My wretched silence! Father, forgive me, I knew not what I was doing.

Lear had his Cordelia. I my Anne, who was mother, sister, and chaste lover. Anne, wherever you are, may God bathe you in His love.

Reduced to nothing, Cordelia becomes a queen.
Reduced to nothing, Lear becomes a man.
Reduced to nothing, I become . . .

The turning point of *King Lear* is the king's great soliloquy on the tempestuous heath; it is simply a paraphrase of the Sermon on the Mount—so much for critics who say *King Lear* is not Christian in its philosophy.

Lear finally realizes that he was not a good king, or more simply, a good man:

> Poor naked wretches, wheresoe'er you are,
> That bide the pelting of this pitiless storm,
> How shall your houseless heads and unfed sides,
> Your looped and windowed raggedness defend you
> From seasons such as these? O, I have ta'en
> Too little care of this.

Was I not one of the wretches of the London streets? How many fevers and chills from the pelting of storms? And always I was in the presence of those more impoverished than I. I think of the women barely beyond being lasses and their children who were abandoned to the streets. Oh, that our Queen would descend from her gilded coach and walk the streets of her city and see her people; she could only return to Buckingham Palace with a heavy heart and pray Lear's prayer.

Elizabeth appears before my mind's eye. Houseless and husbandless, she had one offspring, a golden child named Julia. So frail, the child died in midwinter in the shadow of

Parliament. Elizabeth calmly carried her to the Thames' edge and stuffed stones in the child's little empty pockets and placed her in the water as though the Thames were the sacred Ganges. Down she floated and disappeared. Only then did Elizabeth speak—"She is now safe with Jesus"—and wept like all mothers since the dawn of time.

Self-knowledge is the turning point in all literature, in all lives. When we finally see our true selves, we can do only one of two things: deny the truth, like Oedipus Rex, or learn compassion, like Lear. Blindness or insight. Thank you, Jesus, for sending me the insight that does not blind but illuminates.

The paradox of opium: its seeming promise was to open the doors of perception, when, in fact, it closed them. I think of poor Coleridge and his meager poetic opus. Had he not succumbed to opium, he'd have been our most prolific poet. I must always remember his fate—or it will be mine.

April 1

Today Sebastian and I walked to the Field of the Cross, where upon a mound stands a huge crucifix with a life-size corpus of Jesus. We stood before it in prayer for I know not how long. Then we went to Sebastian's bench and sat in the sunlight. I shivered in the April wind.

"My son, are you well?"

His compassion moved me.

"I am better. I can eat again. I can read again. I can walk a mile or two without exhaustion. Yes, I am better."

"Are you happy here?"

Happiness vanished the day my mother died. If she had lived, perhaps my life would have been different. But then again, the security of my mother's love and my father's home would have imprisoned me. In a fit of anger against my father I departed my home forever. I never stole laudanum, never! Although I purchased it with father's hard-earned money—I'm ashamed to admit. Oh, Father, you possessed many valid reasons for your wrath, but I never pilfered your laudanum.

Father deserved a better son.

"Yes, Father, I am happy here." Sebastian smiled and took my hand in his and made the sign of the Cross on my palm.

As we walked back to the Priory, I explained to Father my fascination with Shakespeare's theme of nothingness. The Fool says boldly to Lear, "Now thou art an O without a figure. I am better than thou art now. I am a Fool. Thou art nothing."

"To be reduced to nothing is the only way some learn", I said, thinking of myself.

"Yes, Francis, many of us must be reduced to nothing," Sebastian agreed, "and then we must pass through the zero, which is likened to Christ's crown of thorns; few pass unscathed." He squeezed my arm in reassurance. "But never fear; Christ heals all wounds." We passed the remainder of the way in silence that was not a silence but a plenitude of mutual understanding.

April 5

Gloucester's bloody eyepits, the fiendish work of Lear's son-in-law, haunted me throughout the night! Everywhere I looked I beheld those blood-soaked holes! He had cause to wish for death until Edgar tricked him into life. "Thy life's a miracle", Edgar said to his father as he awakened from his swoon. He lied to offer hope to his father.

Being pagans, neither Lear nor Gloucester could fully understand that without a Good Friday, there is no Easter; without a Cross, no empty tomb; without death, no Resurrection.

I met a child today, a child with great candor of eyes. She had been gathering wildflowers and offered them to me. I was inexpressibly touched and pleased. I spoke to her gently; she confidently spoke of the flowers, the birds, and brothers and sisters—nothing, surely, to interest any man, yet I listened, enchanted. How simple and strange and wonderful and sweet. All this exquisiteness ordinary men take for granted, like the daisies they trample underfoot, knowing not what daisies are to him whose feet have wandered in grime.[1]

I have composed a poem! It appeared full-blown in my mind, all sixty verses. I hastened to Brother Placid, who swiftly found me pen, ink, and paper. It concerns the child I met on the road. Its title, "Daisy".

Daisy

> Where the thistle lifts a purple crown
>   Six foot out of the turf,
> And the harebell shakes on the windy hill—
>   O the breath of the distant surf!—

The hills look over on the South,
    And southward dreams the sea;
And with the sea-breeze hand in hand
    Came innocence and she.

Where 'mid the gorse the raspberry
    Red for the gatherer springs,
Two children did we stray and talk
    Wise, idle, childish things.

She listened with big-lipped surprise,
    Breast-deep mid flower and spine:
Her skin was like a grape whose veins
    Run snow instead of wine.

She knew not those sweet words she spake,
    Nor knew her own sweet way;
But there's never a bird, so sweet a song
    Thronged in whose throat that day.

Oh, there were flowers in Storrington
    On the turf and on the spray;
But the sweetest flower on Sussex hills
    Was the Daisy-flower that day!

Her Beauty smoothed earth's furrowed face.
    She gave me tokens three:—
A look, a word, of her winsome mouth,
    And a wild raspberry.

A berry red, a guileless look,
    A still word,—strings of sand!
And they made my wild, wild heart
    Fly down to her little hand.

For standing artless as the air,
   And candid as the skies,
She took the berries with her hand,
   And the love with her sweet eyes.

The fairest things have fleetest end,
   Their scent survives their close:
But the rose's scent is bitterness
   To him that loved the rose.

She looked a little wistfully,
   Then went her sunshine way:—
The sea's eye had a mist on it,
   And the leaves fell from the day.

She went her unremembering way,
   She went and left in me
The pang of all the partings gone,
   And partings yet to be.

She left me marvelling why my soul
   Was sad that she was glad;
At all the sadness in the sweet,
   The sweetness in the sad.

Still, still I seemed to see her, still
   Look up with soft replies,
And take the berries with her hand,
   And the love with her lovely eyes.

Nothing begins, nothing ends,
   That is not paid with moan;
For we are born in other's pain,
   And perish in our own.

Easter. Christ is risen!

At Lauds I watched the stained-glass window of Christ become a sun-pierced icon of emerald, ruby, and sapphire. Without the sunlight, the window is lifeless. With the sunlight, it is transformed into the Light of the world. How proper and fitting was today's sunrise!

My own darkened life has here at Storrington been irradiated by the light of the lives of these holy monks. Their faces are icons of Christ, radiant with His love and compassion. How fortunate I am to abide among them.

When I gaze upon Father Sebastian's face, I am gazing upon Christ. "Our faces are forged within the soul", he once said to me on one of our afternoon walks. How else explain the sublimity and dignity and repose of such a face as his?

Faces and therefore eyes. I shall never forget the day I looked into Sebastian's eyes and felt that Christ was gazing at me. Under his gaze I became myself.

When on the rare occasion I look upon myself in a mirror, I no longer see the dreamy young man of full mouth, clear eyes, and unwrinkled brow. I see a face ravaged by opium, aged beyond its years, a face that looked upon the abyss and was terrified. Such terror leaves a permanent mark. I only hope that when others gaze upon me they won't be frightened.

I have commenced my essay on Shelley. Some of it I composed in the sleepless night. Until I was twenty-two I studied Shelley more than any other poet. If one looks closely and penetrates his wild mask of revolutionary metaphysics, one finds a child's face; thus his poetry is verse of make-believe.

But can I do justice to Shelley? Is my brain capable of thinking? Writing verse and criticism are two very different ways of movement. One is a gamboling and the other a plodding. Already my nerves are on edge, but I shall combat my nature, for only in composition do I lose myself, do I achieve a modicum of Pax.

It is midnight. Why has sound sleep not returned? Remorse for my sins? My horrid London memories? Or the fearful opium still lingering in the maze of my mind, like London's shrouded mists?

Perhaps I should now make my general confession. Do I have the courage?

I sit in the monastic silence of this cell, reading Shakespeare. Lear dearly enfolds Cordelia in his arms. A pagan Pietà. He has no consolation in faith; thus, he utters the saddest words in all English literature, "Thou'lt come no more / Never, never, never, never, never." Who but Shakespeare would dare such repetition?

April 15

The essay on Shelley progresses. Shelley's painful youth at school. How the sensitive boy was tortured! "Nothing begins, and nothing ends / That is not paid with moan." My essay is, I am certain, a breakthrough. Wilfrid and Alice will be surprised and, I hope, delighted. It is far greater than "Paganism Old and New", which I wrote under the most trying conditions. It is a miracle that it was written and salvaged, albeit in soiled raiment, being my constant companion on the streets. Much of it I composed in Anne's little haven of a room, with its stone floor and low light. My dear, poor Anne, my sad Semele, whom I have not seen since the day I told her my poem *Passion of Mary* was published. Often, since, have I longed to encounter her, to thank her for that graciously delicate whisper that brought such healing to my hurt, indignant heart. But I never shall, till the day that evens all debts. It is not likely that these lines will ever have meeting with her sweet, sad eyes. Could that be, I would desire she might read in them a gratitude that passes speech and the accumulated silences of many intervening years.[2]

> Who clasp lost spirits, also clasp their hell;
> You have clasped, and burn, sad child, sad Semele!
> One half of my cup have you drunk too well,
> And that's the death; the immortality
> Girt in the fiery spirit flies your lip.
> That to my deathless progeny of pain
> You should be mother, bear your fellowship
> I' the mortal grief, without the immortal gain!
> Not only I, that these poor verse live,
> A heavy vigil keep of parchèd nights;
> But you for unborn men your pangs must give,
> And wake in tears that they may dream delights.
> What poems be, Sweet, you did never know;
> And yet are poems suckled by your woe.

April 18

The following required a full day of pushing my brain, but I am proud of it and only hope it captures the brightness of

41

Shelley's wings and the lift of his swift flight and the innocence of his wondrous face.

The same thing is conspicuous throughout his singing; it is the child's faculty of make-believe to the *n*th power. He is still at play, save only that his play is such as manhood stops to watch, and his playthings are those that the gods give their children. The universe is his box of toys. He dabbles his fingers in the dayfall. He is gold-dusty with tumbling amidst the stars. He makes bright mischief with the moon. The meteors nuzzle their noses in his hand. He teases into growling the kennelled thunder and laughs at the shaking of its fiery chain. He dances in and out of the gates of heaven: its floor is littered with his broken fancies. He runs wild over the fields of ether. He chases the rolling world. He gets between the feet of the horses of the sun. He stands in the lap of patient Nature and twines her loosened tresses after a hundred willful fashions to see how she will look nicest in his song.[3]

I do not believe Shelley maintained his atheism. I cannot prove this, only believe it intuitively. His was a religion of humanity. Shelley, my brother . . .

April 20

A day of sunlight and cool breezes. Today I ventured beyond the Field of the Cross to the foot of Jacob's Ladder, a steep winding path into the hills. When I looked up its vistaed height, I became dizzy. Although I longed to climb, especially for the promised view of Sussex, I decided it is too soon for such an ascent.

My presence disturbed a flock of rooks, rising suddenly

and rushing into flight toward the Downs. Birds and poets go hand in hand. Shelley's skylark, Keats' nightingale, Rossetti's songbirds. My bird? Poe's raven. Poor Poe; they dismissed his genius as madness. Is not all genius tinged with madness?

I am so blessed to abide in this Garden of Eden, this Priory of Pax. The monks are icons of Christ. They speak French and a little English. Fortunately I retain my French and have no difficulty communicating.

I am, however, no Adam, as I explained to Father Sebastian this morning after his beautiful Mass. I am Peter, not the beloved John. I betrayed my Jesus and his dear Mother not thrice, not seven times seven, but seven times seventy times. How many thousands of drops of laudanum? I cannot plumb the river of laudanum that flowed through my veins for a decade. Every drop turned tear.

At Father Sebastian's instigation I narrated my first Resurrection. A man named McMaster, such a goodly man, espied me one dull November day as I walked in a daze near Leicester Square. Through London's cacophony of men and horses and coaches a voice reached me, saying, "Is your soul saved?" I focused my eyes upon him. A short, stout man with a kindly face stared at me. He was an evangelical well known to assist the downtrodden, a member of Saint Martin-in-the-Field.

"By what right do you ask this question?" I said.

He smiled, and we talked. I explained to him that I was a Catholic; it did not in the least disturb my kind angel, who offered me shelter and a job in his bootshop. He said, "If you won't let me save your soul, let me save your body."

"God bless him", Father Sebastian said. "He was surely sent to you by our Blessed Lord."

"Yes, and I again betrayed Him."

For six months I vanquished my opium imbibing and began to compose my essay on paganism and Christianity. The first months were hell, but my mind found haven by fixing itself upon my conviction that only on the wings of Christianity arrived the great truth that love is a marriage of body and soul. Then the piercing insight: the pagans never understood the beauty of a woman's eyes, to which they never alluded. You'll find no Beatrice in pagan verse.

I wrote all this down in my essay, which I finally titled "Paganism Old and New"; it greatly impressed Wilfrid, who remarked on our first meeting (how mortified I was of my lamentable appearance!), "You must have had access to many books when you wrote that essay."

I said, "That is precisely where the essay fails. I had no books by me at the time, save Aeschylus and Blake." I had been expelled from both Guildhall Library and the British Reading Room. I could not blame them, for I looked like a Bedlam madman. And too many of us poor were using their washrooms for ablutions.

I remember McMaster's eyes on the day he asked me to leave. They were not accusatory, but saddened. He said that I was his only failure. My own father could have said the same.

When I left McMaster, I dropped my essay in the letter box of *Merry England*. Next day I spent my last halfpenny on two boxes of matches and began the struggle for life.

That fateful day I ended my letter to Wilfrid with these words: "Kindly address your rejection to the Charing Cross Post Office. Yours with little hope."

May 1

I sat the night staring through my casement at the insane eye of the moon. The opium in my drawer repeatedly whis-

44

pered to me. My hand reached out to the drawer's handle. After beseeching Mary Immaculate for a half hour, I was able to resist one more time.

Today I finished "Shelley". I composed it with my tears. Perhaps Catholic readers may be shy about his life's shadows. But I shall not change one word, not one comma.

Vespers. When my eyes adjusted to the dim chapel, I saw that I was surrounded by locals, all in various postures of prayer: four kneeling on the floor, two fingering rosary beads, others sitting in their stalls with their heads bowed, still as statues. The rest gazed at the candle-illuminated tabernacle at the front of the church, their lips moving in silent prayer.

There is a sanctity in stillness, the kind of stillness one never finds in London—except in a few of the more ancient chapels, whose very stones foster silent adoration.

We silently waited for the twilight Office to begin. The silence was soothing, and I luxuriated in it. This is the same silence that unnerved me when I was a boy and believed God was regarding me in my every thought and movement. No, I'd remind myself, there is no escape from God. But then I bewitched myself to believe in escape and nearly destroyed myself by self-delusions.

The rustling robes and soft slaps of sandals against marble floor announced the monks' arrival; one by one they came. Tall, elegant Father Angus ambled like a king, his family's wealth and the best schools indelibly stamped upon him; stately Brother Augustine, serene as a swan, measured us all before he shifted his gaze upon the golden tabernacle gleaming in the candlelight. He dropped to both his knees while his white-sleeved arms flew into the air and then descended as palms joined in an arrow of prayer. In the world of the theater his gesture would be deemed histrionic, but here it is utterly humble. Brother Jerome's entry was deliberate and cautious, and he patted his stall seat several times, then lifted it and knelt in the U-shaped space. Old Father Sebastian arrived; his ancient face and grave mien were like those of an Old Testament prophet. He has the face of a man who has seen beyond the veil. He must surely be near ninety. Monastic life, with its rhythm, silence, solitude, and diet forbidding meat and eggs, surely promotes longevity.

Every monk enfolded in a white cloud of cowl and habit: hundreds of years of history contained in their every white movement . . .

May 3

Father Sebastian's face proclaims an ineffable holiness. At this morning's Mass his ancient holy hands held the Body and Blood of Christ. Those very hands prepared my breakfast. He poured my milk into my tea and buttered my bread. My own hands trembled due to the fierce temptation of the prior night. Somehow Father intuited my struggle, for when he departed he repeated Wilfrid's encouragement, "You can do it."

May 4

Today Father and I slowly walked to Jacob's Ladder. He is physically stronger than I, who am thirty. At one bend in the path he unconsciously took my arm. He'll never know how his spontaneous, kind gesture nearly moved me to tears. Why does every visitant kindness cause me to weep?

"Tell me about your first published poem."

I explained my lifelong devotion to the Mother of God. I was living at home. It was a Sunday in September when Father Richardson of Saint Mary's, Ashton-under-Lyne, delivered a sermon on "Our Lady of Sorrows". I was so inspired I returned home to write a poem while the Muse was upon me. I kept the poem always with me, even through the horrid days of London. In a last effort to save my poetic dream, I sent it along with my essay on paganism to Wilfrid's *Merry England*. I never heard from him and accepted my rejection until a family friend, Canon Carroll, informed me that my poem had indeed been published in Wilfrid's magazine. I wrote to Wilfrid. Thus began my great friendship with the Meynells.

"Our Lady must love you very much."

"Yes, Mary is always with me." I unbuttoned my shirt collar and lifted my medal of Mary.

"I have worn this for more than ten years. Not once have I taken it off. I was without socks, shirt, and good shoes, had sold everything I owned for laudanum. But I never forsook this medal. Yes, Father, our Lady loves me. It is appropriate that my first poem be dedicated to her."

"Recite it for me, Francis."

In my weakened voice I began,

> O Lady Mary, thy bright crown
> Is no mere crown of majesty;
> For with the reflex of His own
> Resplendent thorns Christ circled thee.
>
> The red rose of this Passion-tide
> Doth take a deeper hue from thee,
> In the five wounds of Jesus dyed,
> And in thy bleeding thoughts, Mary!

I advanced as far as the third stanza before I wept. Sebastian patted me on the arm, and we continued on in silence.

If Wilfrid and Alice had not published my poem, I later told him, I would have died among the great mass of London's impoverished—alone.

Oh, the humiliation of my first meeting with Wilfrid! I remember the assistant's shock when he looked upon me. Was there a figure in all of London more ragged and unkempt than I? No shirt, my coat of holes, my feet bare in broken shoes, unshaved, and malodorous. How ashamed I felt. But when Wilfrid saw me, he saw not my windowed raggedness: he saw the poet. For that I am eternally grateful. I may have lost a father, but I also gained one. Thanks be to Thee, Jesus.

May 10

Today I was caught in a torrential rain. Like Lear I railed against the elements. There was not a hovel nearby for shelter. By the time I returned to the Priory, I was drenched to my skin and now will likely be struck down by pneumonia.

Oh, my dear Jesus, what more?

May 12

A severe chill, not pneumonia. But I am confined to my room, which is a penance. My only boon when on the streets of London was my lack of confinement. I walked everywhere and knew London like the palm of my hand.

I am rereading *King Lear*.

I am moved to tears by Edgar's loving care of his father. Edgar arrayed as poor ol' Tom leading his blinded father to the cliffs of Dover. His raison d'être to prevent his father's suicide. "Why I do trifle thus with his despair / Is done to cure it."

Father Sebastian is my Edgar, a reversal of roles that humbles me. Today he came to my cell. I sat on my bed, he in the chair. The room was flooded with sunlight. He reminded me that God's love is unconditional, that no matter what I have done in the past or what I shall do in the future, God loves me. He said that although I might flee from God, God would seek me to the ends of the earth.

Why am I comforted by such? Perhaps because my own dear father never went in search of me. He gave me up for dead. But he had warned me on that dreadful day, "If you walk out that door, I shall not come after you. It's your decision." I cannot blame him; he overlooked much, always allowing another chance. But he was wrong about my stealing. If only he had believed me—but how could he when I had lied so many times?

May 15

God's grace: two ideas for poems have suddenly appeared. One about the sun and my sweet crucified Jesus. The other so strange an image I shall not yet write it down, but I found it in Shelley. Perhaps it is too strange, too bizarre, too daring. But why does my heart leap at the very thought?

During the night I awakened to find my Anne sitting in my chair, lovingly gazing at me. She was young and beautiful, arrayed in a white, silken gown. Her golden hair was long and braided. Her eyes overflowed with love—for me, unworthy me! When I ventured to speak, she lifted her lovely finger to her lips, saying, "Hush." In silence we gazed at one another. Time disappeared. Then she arose from her seat and came to me and kissed my brow. She said, "Remember me in your poetry." Remember you? How could I ever forget the sweetest soul I have ever known?

May 20

A beautiful May day. After Mass I remained in the sanctuary and knelt before the statue of Mary, "O tender Lady, Queen Mary." I prayed for all those I love. I prayed until my knees hurt. Then I was inspired to walk to Jacob's Ladder. It begins in stone steps and widens into a path that meanders to a chalk mine and then continues on to the summit, which I reached after an hour of climbing.

The sight of the distant surf and the beautiful, fertile valley beneath was worth the effort. Three men working in the fields looked like midgets. On my way up I stopped several times to appreciate the grandeur of the beauty before me. The Priory looked small but peaceful and inviting. In the distance I observed a mist dissipate to reveal a range of hills.

I felt not exhausted but rather exhilarated. A good sign that my health is returning. Now if only the remnant mist upon my mind will lift. Although I must admit my mind is finally moving, finally working. Thus far I have completed one poem, my essay on Shelley, and gleams of two poems have pierced my soul.

Wilfrid is wise. Poetry cannot be composed unless one can hear the "still, small voice". I would venture to say that silence and solitude are the sine qua non of being a poet.

I am not afraid of being alone. Loneliness accosted me when I was young—and won me for life.

I have begun my poem "Ode to the Setting Sun". The first verses arrived as I stood in the Field of the Cross under the shadow of the crucifix. As the sun, a bubble of fire, began its descent, a single ray of light illuminated the face of Christ Crucified. Ah, me!

The sun is the symbol of Christ. This is not new, but I shall present it newly. As the sun offers life through light, so am I filled with life (and a strange passion) in composing this poem.

After Vespers I met Father Sebastian in the cool, still cloister.

"Francis, your face glows." There was no innuendo in his voice; he would have known if I had relapsed.

"Father, I am writing verse, and I believe it is the best I have ever composed."

"God be praised! I shall pray for you, Francis. I shall pray that your poem will lead you toward the Light of the World, Who is Christ."

Such a coincidence! Surely I am in the hands of the Lord.

A week of joy! My nights are full of sleep's balm. During the morning I worked on my ode. Never before have images poured forth so freely; never before have I experienced such joy in the act of creation. It is as if a shroud has been lifted from my mind.

My desire for opium has vanished. I forgot its existence in my desk and only remembered it when I realized that my ode is completely free of opium's influence. No Kubla Khan is my ode! It is the pure creation of my imagination, of my soul.

My ode is completed. An inner voice warns me that perhaps it is too gorgeous, too encrusted with gems, too violent in its diction. My reservations come too late, for I promised myself that I would post it tomorrow to Wilfrid and Alice. They will recognize whether or not it is worthy.

But in my bones I believe it is the best I have thus far written.

> The wailful sweetness of the violin
> Floats down the hushèd waters of the wind,
> The heart-strings of the throbbing harp begin
> To long in aching music. Spirit-pined,
>
> In wafts that poignant sweetness drifts, until
> The wounded soul ooze sadness. The red sun,
> A bubble of fire, drops slowly toward the hill,
> While one bird prattles that the day is done.
>
> O setting Sun, that as in reverent days
> Sinkest in music to thy smoothèd sleep,
> Discrowned of homage, though yet crowned with rays,
> Hymned not at harvest more, though reapers reap:
>
> For thee this music wakes not. O deceived,
> If thou hear in these thoughtless harmonies
> A pious phantom of adorings reaved,
> And echo of fair ancient flatteries!
>
> Yet, in this field where the Cross planted reigns,
> I know not what strange passion bows my head
> To Thee, whose great command upon my veins
> Proves thee a god for me not dead, not dead!

For worship it is too incredulous,
    For doubt—oh, too believing—passionate!
What wild divinity makes my heart thus
    A fount of most baptismal tears?—Thy straight

Long beam lies steady on the Cross. Ah me!
    What secret would thy radiant finger show?
Of thy bright mastership is this the key?
    Is this thy secret, then? And is it woe?

Fling from thine ear the burning curls, and hark
    A song thou has not heard in Northern day;
For Rome too daring, and for Greece too dark,
    Sweet with wild wings that pass, that pass away!

The secret to life's enigma is daily before us in the rising and setting sun; in Christ's death and Resurrection. I too was dead and now live. Dear Jesus, thank You for my rebirth.

June 4

In the parlor of the retreat house awaiting the dawn, I sat in a red leather armchair, a cup of black coffee warm in my palms. It is a beautiful room of dark wainscoting, rich carpet, and comfortable wingbacks, all gifts from wealthy patrons. The east window promised a panoramic view of the awakening Downs.

The sun slowly rose; it wasn't a sudden, blinding illumination. The eye had time to adjust to the initial hues of gold and pink and violet—suffused tones, not glaring. The hills and meadows gradually assumed form in the glory of light. The shadows, too, played their part, providing the contrast necessary for clarity.

Father Sebastian remarked that the monastic life is like the dawn: "Expect no sudden light, only a gradual enlightenment over time."

Silence enfolded me.

The need for silence led me here to this remote monastery. On our first meeting Father Sebastian warned me, "Silence is the sine qua non of the contemplative life . . . if silence frightens you, then you'll not be happy here."

I placed my cup on the mahogany table, next to my closed Psalter. The cup, the book, the table: we basked in the first light.

As happy as I am, I could not live here for the rest of my life; London is too much in my bones . . . for better or for worse.

In the meantime I live humbly here at the Priory, ever thankful for Pax. I watch cloudbanks, the sunrise, and the sunset. I listen to birds awaken in the morning and grow quiet in the evening. I take walks and cast my gaze on flowers and trees. Yes, a humble life.

The time is ripe ("Ripeness is all!") to confess my sin to Father Sebastian. When he handed me a copy of Saint Augustine's *Confessions*, I understood his silent urging. Yes, I must seek to be absolved. I must tell him about Timothy. Poor Timothy! If I had not been ensnared by opium, the poor boy would have lived . . . I am desperate to be absolved of his death.

Then and only then shall I receive the Eucharist.

By now my ode must be in Wilfrid and Alice's hands. I eagerly await their reactions. To prevent anxiety, I have focused all my attention upon Shelley's "Heaven's Winged Hound". A poem about God as hound: Would it be blasphemous? If not, I shall follow the hound wherever it leads me. Or rather, wherever it hounds me!

I have not felt this lighthearted since . . . since I first read Saint Augustine in Latin. Like Augustine I wasted my youth—not in the sins of the flesh as he but in the excesses of the imagination, but they are sins nevertheless. "Oh, Beauty so old and so new, too late I have loved thee!"

This is the greatest day of my life, for my dear friends Wilfrid and Alice have proclaimed my genius.

When they arrived this morning I was shocked and raced to them, fearing something had happened to the children. But when I saw their faces radiant, I knew it was good news. And the good news was my ode!

Wilfrid embraced me. "Francis, we have come to praise you and your poem. You bowled us over!"

"Yes, Francis, it is an ode of great spiritual beauty", Alice said, taking my hand and squeezing it. Oh, if she knew how much her touch meant to me: it was paradise.

We sat in the refectory, where Brother Placid feasted us with tea, cakes, and freshly made bread. Wilfrid and I ate heartily, but Alice picked like the beautifully exquisite bird she is.

"We hope for more from you, Francis", Wilfrid said.

"There will be more. I'm already embarked on another

ode", I said, smiling, and my heart full of happiness at this unexpected and joyous visitation.

"Tell us about it", Alice said, her lovely blue eyes filled with curiosity. If the eyes are the windows of the soul, then there is not a more beautiful soul in all the world than Alice; she is my Beatrice, who inspires me in my verse.

"I cannot breathe a word of it, or it may disappear", I said, waving my hand like Prospero.

"Give us a hint", teased Alice.

"No, I shan't tell, for I want it to be your Christmas gift."

"We must wait till Christmas!" Wilfrid exclaimed. "That's unfair of you, Francis."

"But I do have something for you now." And I handed to them my poem "Daisy".

They read it, huddled together like the lovers they are. After finishing, they looked at me and were silent. I momentarily became anxious, afraid my verse was inferior, until I noticed their moist eyes. Each embraced me.

"You are a great poet", Alice said. I could no longer hold back the floodgate of tears. A man of thirty, I have at last heard what I have always longed to hear—and from a great poet herself.

In the night I could not sleep, but I was not plagued. Alice's beautiful, spiritualized face, with musing saddened eyes, appeared before my mind's eye. There is nothing weak or poetish about her face, only mournful sweetness. Her face is as beautiful as any of her poems.

Inspired by her declaration "you are a great poet", which is engraved upon my heart, I have written a poem in her honor.

In Her Paths

And she has trod before me in these ways!
I think that she has left here heavenlier days;
    And I do guess her passage, as the skies
        Of holy Paradise
        Turn deeply holier,
And, looking up with sudden new delight,
One knows a seraph-wing has passed in flight.
The air is purer for her breathing, sure!
        And all the fields do wear
        The beauty fallen from her;
The winds do brush me with her robe's allure.
'Tis she has taught the heavens to look sweet
        And they do but repeat
The heaven, heaven, heaven of her face!
The clouds have studied going from her grace!
The pools whose marges had forgot the tread
Of Naiad, disenchanted, fled,
        A second time must mourn,
        Bereaven and forlorn.
Ah, foolish pools and meads! You did not see
Essence of old, essential pure as she.
For this was even that Lady, and none other
The man in me calls, 'Love,' the child calls
        'Mother.'

June 9

My life was thrice transformed. I was Christ accosted at
fourteen. At eighteen I read De Quincey's *Confessions of an
Opium-Eater.* Let no one underestimate the power of the
written word to metamorphose a life. William Blake, my

poetical companion throughout my London nightmare, said it best: "We become what we behold."

Then the third event: my meeting with Wilfrid and Alice. I would have disappeared among the faceless people of the abyss had it not been for these guardian angels.

Thank you, dear Mother Mary and my sweet Jesus.

June 10

Wilfrid has asked me for an essay on *Macbeth* for the *Dublin Review*. Oh, to enter Macbeth's gloom-shrouded nightmare: Am I prepared for such a journey? If only it had been *Lear*. Oh, how *Lear* moved me to tears! Yes, Lear died, but he died having been reunited with his beloved Cordelia. Perhaps someday I shall again behold my Anne—then I shall expire happily.

Endured the morning reading *Macbeth*. It is terrifying: he sacrifices his eternal jewel for the golden round. The fool! My argument is new: Lady Macbeth committed regicide before her husband—because she willed it before he. How the critics will howl!

June 11

Macbeth's fatal flaw is not ambition, as commonly concluded. No, it is his possession of an imagination encouraged to run amok. Was I not so plagued when I was under the influence of opium?

Macbeth's and Lady Macbeth's nightmares are ample proof that they are both essentially good; otherwise they'd have not lost a wink of sleep after Duncan's foul and blood-soakened murder. They suffer from ineffable guilt. He says, "Will all great Neptune's ocean wash this blood clean from my hand?" She says, "All the perfumes of Arabia will not sweeten this little hand." Only Christ's dear loving Blood can wash them clean again.

When Macbeth demands the doctor heal his wife, the physician says, "Therein the patient must minister to himself." Both need to drop to their human knees to express their contrition and ask for God's forgiveness; therein lies the cure.

Macbeth's golden round becomes the empty zero, the tale told by an idiot, full of sound and fury, signifying nothing. That is where imagination fails: before nothingness imagination pales.

June 12

I lay awake the night with dyspepsia. During my great poverty I hungered for food, would stand in front of shop windows gazing longingly at puddings and pies kept hot by steam arising from perforated metal. I had not enough to purchase a pennyworth of food.

Now I can eat as much as I desire, but my lacerated stomach is so damaged I can eat only small portions of food of the most bland sort—anything rich and I'm awake the night.

Timothy appeared to me last night. He sat in the very chair where Anne sat. His ever-so-kind eyes chastised me, and then he whispered, "Why, Francis, did you not stop me?" I was chilled to the bone and broke into a cold sweat. He had all the eternal right to ask that terrifying question. Why had I allowed it? His death has haunted me for three years. How shall I ever be able to tell Father Sebastian?

I can never receive the Eucharist until I confess my sin. Never until then.

This morning as the sun rose I found my way to the stream. Sitting on the bank, I silently watched the birds and ducks come and go. Then a doe quietly arrived at water's edge for refreshment. I didn't move. Sleek coated, with a belly plump from summer's plenty, she was unaware of me. Every so often she'd lift her head to listen, to smell, to take measure of her surroundings. She seemed puzzled, repeatedly sniffing the air. When satisfied there was no danger, she returned to drinking. Then, in a shift of breeze, my presence was known. With her head raised, she remained still, only her eyes moving until I was found. For the longest time the doe gazed at me. One long look without blinking. It seemed like an eternity as I held my breath. Then she pranced sideways and vanished into the woods.

A hush descended upon me, and I was beyond silence, beyond thought, beyond time . . .

Ah, the simple things that make life happy: a clean room, a fire in the cold morning, a pipe of tobacco, and books. I have all these here at the Priory.

How I loathed the doss houses! The poor man's hotel. Hotel—what a euphemism! No privacy, no air, only the snores from neighbors in adjacent pigeonhole cells with their paper-thin walls. And the smells! How degrading and unwholesome are such places. I learned to prefer London's alleyways and parks.

Brother Placid brings to me all the paper and ink I need. But more than this, he brings to me Christ, Who shines forth from his eyes. Brother Placid's gentleness outgentles all the other good monks.

He is curious about my poem.

"Are you writing about a dog?" he asked.

"Ah, you've been peeking at my papers."

He blushes. "I couldn't help seeing your title."

"No, dear Placid, my poem is about God. But I use a hound as a metaphor."

He laughs and departs shaking his head. Will others react in the same fashion? Nevertheless, I shall continue to the end, for this ode is to be my autobiography. I cannot equal Augustine's prose, but my verse will stand alongside his *Confessions*. I sound prideful, but I'm not, because my gift is Godgiven.

Augustine and I have much in common. I too loved my mother, who feared for my soul. I too fled from God, Who pursued me even into London sewers, where I once sought refuge from the cold.

My health improves. No sore throat, no gum bleeding. My cough is a mere echo of what it was. I breathe more easily. I now walk five miles a day. My shoes are proof! Brother Placid remarked on my improved appetite as I consumed everything he placed before me at dinner.

Today I confessed to Father Sebastian. He has patiently waited five months. Oh, to be relieved of this too onerous burden!

I met Sebastian in the monastic garth beneath an oak tree. He kindly agreed to hear me outside the confessional. My fear of enclosed space prevents any confession in a box. I told him about Timothy.

Timothy was sixteen and well versed in the ways of the London streets. He was a master pickpocket. One day, as I was walking through Charing Cross, I spotted a golden sovereign on the pavement. So did Timothy, and with the grace of a dancer he bent down to scoop it before I had time to open my fingers. In an instant the coin was securely enfolded in his palm.

He looked at me and grinned. Oh, how I could have wept for my slowness. I had not eaten in days, and it was the middle of a particularly frigid winter. He saw my disappointment, my sorrow, my utter poverty—and he took pity on me.

"Come, I'll share half with thee." His voice was refined, and the use of "thee" suggested he was a Quaker. We ate well that day and slept in a doss house on the coldest evening of the year.

We became fast friends, for Timothy loved verse as I did. We would share our favorite poems from memory and debate who was the greatest poet. I fought for Shelley, he for Keats, in whom he saw himself, as he too was short in stature and ever a fighter.

He was also an opium eater, and we both aided one another down that path; neither of us went without the dreadful drug when the other was in possession.

Later, I learned that Timothy was indeed raised in a

Quaker household. But he was not one for turning the cheek and often became embroiled in fisticuffs, which led to a disagreement with his parents. He left home and soon learned the ways of the streets and to support himself through theft.

One mild December day we spent our last on a bottle of laudanum, imbibing in a park not far from Charing Cross. Timothy was melancholic—pining for his home and parents—and voiced his threat to take his own life. I laughed, thinking he was making jest, as he was wont to do. But in the swiftest movement he removed his belt and hanged himself from the nearby tree. I watched him swing for the longest time.

"I made no effort to help him."

"But it's not your fault, Francis. You were under the influence of opium."

"I should've stopped him . . . I've committed grave sin."

"Sin is grave when it is willed. You did not will his death, for your will wasn't free."

"But Father, his soul is forever damned because I stood by and did nothing."

"Do not presume to know the ways of God. Contrition occurs in a breath. Now, is there anything else that keeps you from Christ?"

I unfolded my life to the present, and he absolved me of my transgressions, and I instantly felt as light as a fledgling's feather.

Tomorrow for the first time in several years I shall receive the Eucharist.

Today I have been reunited with my Jesus. Words are insufficient to express my joy—and I a poet! Suffice to say that not I but Christ lives in me. From His first accosting, He has been my most, my beyond all. Though I became lost, I was at all time in his gaze, He in front and behind . . .

Today I awakened to a chorus of birds, whose singing, piping, trilling, and grace notes inspire me to sing God's praise with similar passion—and joy.

Therein lies the poet's (and the mystic's) dilemma—to find joy in the gloom, brightness in the darkness. Was not my gloom, after all, shade of His hand, outstretched caressingly?

I slept not a wink until I hammered out the final draft of the first stanza of *The Hound of Heaven*. The first stanza contains my whole life, my journey to this moment in Storrington. I chart my flight from Christ with all my escape routes, which are not escape routes, for there is no escape from the Hound of Heaven.

At midnight I fell asleep. Then to awaken to the Great Silence. This blessed silence! Oh, how mind tormenting was London's noise! The wail of human voices! I cannot ever forget the utterances of the hundreds of men and women, homeless, hungry, dirty, and despairing. They had all rights to lament, but with such speech that should never have been uttered, never have been heard by a living soul, language meant only for the inferno.

Now I hear only the holy prayer of good monks. Thank you, Jesus. May I never again hear Your name blasphemed or taken in vain.

July 15

I progress with the Hound. It is a golden tabernacle draped in purple. The key to its opening is faith. But even the unbeliever will find sustenance. Such is my hope.

July 16

As I write today's date, I am astonished. How many times in London I knew not the day, the week, the month, or even the year? One day was as another. To dawn, I said, "Be sudden", and to eve, "Be soon."

How quickly it all returns. Huddled beneath bridge arches, we rejected men, women, and children of London sought respite from the rain and the snow. Even the rats joined our melancholy company, feeding upon the meager scraps fallen on the filthy mud. So many arches in my life.

> I fled Him, down the nights and down the days;
> I fled Him, down the arches of the years.

July 20

Mass is more beautiful now that I can join the monks in the Eucharist. I was ashamed to be the only one not to receive, proclaiming the state of my soul to all present. Having laid Timothy to rest, I abide in Pax.

Before I take the Host upon my tongue, I offer a prayer for my youthful friend of the streets and hope he is with Thee, gentle Jesus. Timothy's own gentleness is what in the end destroyed him. His swagger and boasting could not veil his true spirit; he was a gentle young man who loved poetry, and for such a love he was mocked. *Requiescat in pace.*

Is not my life's majority contained in this one verse:

> I fled Him, down the labyrinthine ways
> Of my own mind.

When I was young, my mind was as spacious and serene as the interior of a church. Candlelight and stained-glass windows offered poetic illumination. Oh, how I would linger in church, kneeling for hours rapt in—I almost said prayer. But I wasn't praying—I should have been—but I was dreaming. Yes, a dreamy lad who found the world frightening, a lad who longed to escape into meditationment of beauty.

Once, gazing upon our church's stained-glass window of the Good Shepherd, I found myself walking with Christ, gathering His sheep. I helped Him round up all the stray lambs, and after our work was completed, we sat in onement under a cypress tree for a meal of bread, olives, and wine.

When I returned to myself, I discovered that two hours had flown by. Our pastor, Father Ignatius, preparing for Mass, glanced at me and smiled, surely thinking I was a pious boy. No, not pious, only imaginative. The real world never appealed to me except as it is a shadow of the world to come. And yet have I not experienced moments of great ecstasy in the contemplation of nature's beauty?

All that we imagine is based on this real world because it is the locus we know—the only locus. Even my opium-haunted dreams were but fabrications patterned on what I had seen and heard of the world. Which to prefer: A rose in my hand to contemplate or an imagined rose arising from my own mind? I have been sorely tempted to choose imagination's rose, which never withers, never dies . . . Today I'll take in my hand the rose that grew from the earth and bloomed in the air, knowing full well that its scent will fade and its blossoms wither. In order to do so, I need to trust that, like the setting sun, which will arise in the morrow, so too will the rose bloom again.

I must more assiduously devote my attention to the world, for the beauty of my verse depends upon exquisite detail. Oh, how I regret my multitudinous years of inattention.

I have discarded my essay on *Macbeth*. The witches are too real and return to me too many horrific memories. I once observed a trio of women drown a baby in the Thames' murky waters. Whether or not the baby was already dead I never knew, but I swore I heard the child's cry. But in those opium-hazed days of my hallucinated mind I could not distinguish reality from vision. Did I not write a poem *The Ballad of the Witch Babies*? It is submerged in my trunk—I am too frightened to relive such a hell; furthermore, I have no desire to defile this holy place where the name of God is hourly praised, where prayer daily unfolds like a blooming flower.

Macbeth's tragedy is that he believes in nothing. I have never for a moment believed that life is a tale told by an idiot, full of sound and fury, signifying nothing. Never have I lost my conviction that the purpose of my life is to save my soul. I may have fled from this truth, but I never lost my belief in it. I must relay my belief in the Hound. Yes, the Hound shall serve not only as my verse autobiography but also as my testament.

Sunday. Sunday in a monastery is heaven on earth. The silentness is like no other silence. Even the church bells sound muffled in honor of the Sabbath.

The monks look fresh, revived, and although they smile often, they seem to smile the more on this holy day of the week. Brother Placid is even more gentle in his ways, gentle as the Agnus Dei.

Attracted by the sun gleaming on the Downs and the cloudless blue sky, I walked for hours today but did not realize the extent of my walk until I returned to the monastery, where I was greeted by an anxious Brother Placid.

"Francis, we were worried about you. You were gone so long."

"Was I?" I said, perplexed, for I thought I'd been gone for only a short time.

"You left at eleven, and it is now four. You missed lunch."

I was stunned that so much time had fled. I remembered my mother saying, "Francis, you have no sense of time." True. From a young age I was preoccupied with eternity.

The fruit of my walk is honed verse for my Hound.

As I expected, my Shelley essay has been rejected by the *Dublin Review*. Wilfrid and Alice thought the essay splendid, but the editor at *Dublin* is not, I am informed, a Shelley aficionado. It is a setback, but I am too engrossed in the Hound to be disappointed much. The essay will have its day, I am certain.

Shelley is my polestar in poetry, De Quincey in prose. My

poetry, Wilfrid says, reminds him of wafting clouds of incense, and my prose of rich sacerdotal vestments. How well he knows me!

I have spent the afternoon in meditationment of this my verse,

> and in the mist of tears
> I hid from Him, and under running laughter.

In my loneliest moments I wept. I wept where no one could hear or see me. Nearly impossible in London. One day I was so overcome with gloom I sought refuge in the quiet of Saint Etheldreda's church. Empty and dark, it was invitation to weep. I wept until I felt a hand upon my shoulder. I looked up into the kind, concerned face of a Father of Charity. He asked me no questions but offered me food and drink. When I departed, he blessed me.

Even then I longed to confess, to receive the Eucharist. But I was in pursuit of poetry, ignoring God's pursuit of me. I had not yet realized that all beauty is of God and that to have one is to possess the other. This is a truth I have had to learn the arduous way. Thus I rendered my life a Via Dolorosa.

What a sight I must have presented to the priest! Like Edgar, whom Gloucester, his own father, could not recognize, I was dirty, emaciated, and starving. Unshaven and opium soakened, I looked like a madman. I was indeed mad—for opium—and my visions—

A piercing insight from meditating so much upon *King Lear*. Edgar is myself. He negated himself for his father's love and acceptance. Why did Edgar not identify himself until the very end? It can only be that deep within his heart he feared his father's rejection. The filth, the knotted hair, and the howling madness of Tom of Bedlam is Edgar's opinion of himself.

Such revelation is almost too much to bear.

I am ever grateful that I am English for the one reason that I can read Shakespeare in my own tongue. I am again reading *Hamlet*. I feel I know him as well as I know myself. On occasion I feel I am Hamlet. Have I not suffered from the same flaws: indecision and inaction?

Three times I nearly plunged myself into the abyss. But it was not prayer alone that saved me but also Hamlet's meditationment on self-slaughter: "Ay, there's the rub, / For in that sleep of death what dreams may come . . . Must give us pause." "Conscience does make cowards of us all."

I consider Shakespeare's late blank verse to be his highest and most characteristic. Next I shall read *The Tempest*. Prospero learns to forgive his enemies—and himself. Is it not the most difficult mercy, to forgive one's self?

I remember when I was a child of seven, standing in my nightgown before the fire and chattering to my mother. I remember her pulling me up for using a certain word. "That is not used nowadays", she said. "That is one of Shakespeare's words."

"It is, Mamma?" I said, staring at her doubtfully. "But I didn't know it was one of Shakespeare's words!"

"That's just it", she answered. "You have read Shakespeare so much that you are beginning to talk Shakespeare without knowing it. You must take care, or people will think you odd." She was a prophetess. People do think me "odd" and assume that I do on purpose what is often as unconscious as that childish Elizabethanism uttered in my little nightgown before the fire.[4]

I have been abiding on Prospero's island for two days. Dear Anne read to me the whole of *The Tempest* when I was ill. She became my Miranda. She said, with tears in her eyes, "Francis, you are my brave new world." Oh, that I could have been, but she disappeared like Ariel into the thin air.

She had been a governess, but her employer was a lustful man. When she did not relent to his overtures, he ruined her so that no good family would employ her services. Without family and friends, she came to London and followed the only way left to her.

On her shelf lay Shakespeare's plays and the King James Bible, which she read every night on her return home. My dear Anne, my Miranda who ran away from Caliban only to find him in every man she met. I could not be her Ferdinand, but I shall be her Ariel.

What about my own Caliban? Is it not opium, that weaver of sun-drenched dreamscapes? To prefer the dream over the real has from the first been my greatest temptation.

Only when Prospero claims Caliban is he able to free his spirit Ariel: "This thing of darkness I acknowledge mine." Shortly after, Prospero releases Ariel to the elements. Admitting one's darkness is liberating—oh, how tremendously simple it now appears.

There is in this play much wisdom for me to ponder. Only when I admitted my slavery to opium was I able to free my poetic gifts. Only when I confessed my sins was I able to return to my sweet Jesus.

Why is it so difficult to admit wrongdoing? Pride, first my opinion that I was above other mortals and then my opinion that I was below them. At long last I can see the truth about us all: ordinary until touched by God's grace.

I lay awake the night with the worst headpain of my life. Its cause is my overworking on the Hound; the strain has weakened me. My hand reached out to unlock the desk drawer for the longed-for relief. But the Hound repeatedly whispered, "All things betray thee, who betrayest Me." And I again refrained.

I have betrayed my Lord too long, and now I must somehow complete this poem, my life's amendment. I refuse to be a poet of forgetting. I am a poet of remembering and returning. I must be honest about my flight from God, or my ode will be of no worth to the many like me. My ode is didactic, I admit. Is not all art didactic, if only by its announcement that we must attend to the world, to one another, to God?

I arose with the uprisen sun. It was cold enough for a fire. As I lost myself watching the flame, I reflected upon my soul's purgation. A divine purpose has been wrought from my London degradation, for it has become the burning ember with the charcoal of which the Designer Infinite now limns my soul. Yes, soul making ever demands the fire of cleansing, for without it there is no lasting illumination.

> Designer infinite!—
> Ah! must Thou char the wood ere Thou canst limn
>   with it?

Dear Jesus, you who said, "Nolo me tangere", to Mary Magdalen, touch my heart with Your radiant finger so that it beats for one purpose: Thy love.

August 5

Today I had my first visitor other than Wilfrid and Alice. Canon Carroll was my confessor when I was a boy. He is the first to whom I confided my vocational secret: to become a poet. He kept my secret all these years, even during the six terrible years when I attempted to be a doctor—for father.

When he stepped down from the coach, he did so with energy and confidence, those two qualities I always admired in him, the two I always lacked. He was the life of my parents' Sunday meetings. He gave me free rein of the rectory's library, where I feasted my eyes on Shakespeare and all books poetical. He was kind enough to teach me chess, but, more important, he gifted me with a Latin copy of Saint Augustine's *Confessions*, which I forgot in my haste when I left home, but I knew it by heart.

"Francis, you look well."

"Thank you, Father, and you also." We embraced, and I smelled the very same tobacco I had smelled as a boy. He insisted on my leading him to the spot in the Field of the Cross where I was inspired to write my "Ode to the Setting Sun".

"You've read my poem?" I asked, surprised.

"Mr. Meynell shared it with me. Do you mind?"

"No, I'm still not sure when it will be published, but—"

"Of that I can inform you, Francis. It will appear in the September *Merry England*."

"Thank you, Father. That is heartening news. And thank you again for informing me of my first poem. If you hadn't contacted me, well, I don't know what would have become of me."

When we arrived at the cross, Father knelt and prayed. When he finally stood, he looked at me. "All my prayers to Jesus were for you, Francis. I knew when you were a boy there was greatness in you. You have so much now to be thankful for."

As we climbed Jacob's Ladder for the view, Father spoke of my father and asked me to write to him. I agreed, although I expressed my doubt that he would want to hear from me.

"You never understood your father. He loves you more than you know, and he thought he was doing his best by you. But face it, Francis, you were never candid with him; you never told him you had no desire to be a priest or a doctor. Was it fair?"

I was shamed into silence, because I knew in my heart he stated the truth.

We visited my simple room, not much larger than a monk's cell. He especially enjoyed the view from my window. Standing next to my desk, he saw my neatly piled poem.

"*The Hound of Heaven?*"

"Yes, Father. It's my new ode. I've just finished the first draft. It needs refining."

"May I read it?"

I hesitated, more from fear than anything else.

"I won't if you don't want me to", he said, always sensitive to my feelings.

How could I refuse this dear man who along with Wilfrid saved my life?

"I'd be pleased to know your opinion. But I warn you, it's not like anything you've ever read."

Father was lost in a reading that lasted more than a half hour. I observed him closely, hoping to measure his reaction. But his aristocratic face betrayed nothing. He did not sigh or raise an eyebrow or shake his head. He was inscrutable. The longer the time reading, the more anxious I became. Finally I could not bear the tension. "Father, you need not read more if you don't wish to."

He looked up at me and smiled. "Just a few more moments, Francis."

I stared out at the blue sky. It was so quiet I could hear through my open window the trees' rustling.

Father returned the papers to my desktop.

"Francis, your poem is magnificent. That is the only word I can think of. It is a difficult poem, and I will need to read it several more times. But even though I don't understand every verse, I'm powerfully affected, and I truly want to read it again—it's a masterpiece. An opulent jewel of a poem."

"And the Hound? Do you think it's too daring a metaphor for God?"

"Oh, it's daring, but it is also brilliant. I'm not a critic, but I believe your poem will be read a hundred years from now."

I began to tremble. If I had heard these very words from my father, I could have died in the instant a happy death.

Father Carroll came to me and enveloped me in his arms.

"Francis, the beauty of your soul shines from your verse. I predict you will have a great career as a poet. Surely God wants you to be a poet, so you must be faithful to your vocation."

"I should have told my father. He had a right to know I wanted to devote my life to poetry."

"It's not too late to write to him. And if you wish I'll arrange your visit."

I agreed.

We had lunch in the refectory and then attended None. When Father left, he took my face in his hands. "Your poem is great. Be proud of it, Francis. It will be a poem that will help many return to our Lord."

And he was gone . . .

Father Carroll's visitation has returned me to my misspent youth. But would I have learned life's great lesson in any other way, I, a slow learner? I must praise all the pain I have endured, for without it I would not be here now. Without it I would not have composed my poetry. Without inevadable pain and my sweet demon poetry I would have despaired—and died.

Pain, which came to man as a penalty, remains with him as a consecration; by a divine ingenuity, he is permitted to make his ignominy his exaltation. Man, shrinking from pain, is like a child shuddering under his bedcovers and crying, "It is cold!" How many among us, after repeated lessonings of experience, refuse to comprehend that there is no special love without special pain!

Dear Jesus, I thank You for my cross; never permit me to forget its special weight, its power, its saving grace. Never permit me to forget that all that I have lost has been gain, all that I have gained is the cup that runneth over.

I have today received a letter from Wilfrid, who informs me that he sent my prose and poetry to the great Robert

Browning, who wrote back to Wilfrid just before he died. I must record what the eminent poet wrote because I am still incredulous. "Both the verse and the prose are indeed remarkable. . . . Pray assure him, if he cares to know it, that I have a confident expectation of its success, if he will but extricate himself—as by a strenuous effort he may—from all that must now embarrass him terribly."

The idea that in the closing days of his life my writings should have been under his eye and he should have sent me praise and encouragement is one that I shall treasure to the closing days of my life.

September 1

For most of August I worked on completing my Hound. I can now say Finis. I shall post it to Wilfrid tomorrow.

Although I have grown to love the monks here at Storrington, I miss Wilfrid and Alice and the children. I am not meant to be a monk. So I shall request money for my return to London, where I hope I shall continue my career writing for Wilfrid and *Merry England*.

It will be painful to say my good-bye to Father Sebastian, who, because of his age, I shall likely never see again. I dread farewells. For me they have always been final.

September 8

It has taken me a week to muster the courage to meet with Father Sebastian, who is ill in the infirmary. Today Abbot Raines granted me permission to visit him. I did not request to know his ailment, for I'm too afraid to know.

I found him sleeping. His breathing was labored. Late afternoon sunlight beamed upon his face, which even in repose retained a grave dignity. His blankets were undone, so I tucked them in securely. I sat in an armchair to await his awakening.

At midafternoon he opened his eyes and gazed upon me.

"Francis, how good of you to come."

I stood next to his bed.

"Father, I came to say good-bye. I am returning to London, but I could never depart from Storrington without seeing you and receiving your blessing."

He took my hands into his ancient ones and made the sign of the Cross on both my palms. He then asked me to bow my head toward him, and he made the sign of the Cross on my brow.

"Go in peace, Francis. I shall pray for you all the days that are left to me on earth. And you, please, pray for me, for I believe your prayers are precious to Jesus."

"I'll never forget you, Father."

"Nor I you, dear Francis. Remember, you can do it—I am the living proof. Good-bye, my son."

I departed before I made a fool of myself.

Here I sit at my desk to take my last view of the Sussex Downs. I have been happy here in this sanctuary of stillness, and I have accomplished what I had set out to do: to free myself from opium's thralldom. I unlocked the desk and removed the bottle of opium, which I emptied out the window, returning it to the earth from which it arose.

Opium has no allure for me. With God's help I have vanquished all desire for it. And I no longer fear it.

I said farewell to the Abbot. This time Reverend Father did not keep me waiting but ushered me into his office with moving solicitude. I knelt before him for his blessing, and when I bent to kiss his ring, he raised me to my feet and led me to a seat.

"I'm sorry to see you leave", he said, taking a chair behind the desk. "But I understand your desire to resume your life in London. I only hope you were happy with us."

"Thank you, Reverend Father, for I indeed am happy here. But my destiny as a poet lies in London."

He was silent for a long time, a patient silence not eager to be broken. Finally he said, "I want to offer some wisdom, something that will help you in your new life, but I'm at a loss for words."

I smiled to console him, for I fully understand how words do not always arrive when we want or need them.

"Francis, your ode to the sun is a hymn of God's love for his children. It will illuminate many a darkened soul. I can see that you are called to be a poet. Faithfully carry the cross of your vocation, and you will be sanctified through it."

My eyes welled with joyous tears. Were not these the most perfect words he could have uttered?

When I departed I again knelt before him while he placed his consecrated hands upon my head and prayed, "Dear Lord, inspire Francis to compose verse that will remind readers of Your ubiquitous love. In the name of the Father, and of the Son, and of the Holy Ghost."

His last words as I went through the door were "Pax vobiscum." Abbot Raines and Father Sebastian, two men of majestic simplicity, the like of which I've never met and unlikely shall ever meet again.

My stay at Storrington is now ended. But because I love this Priory I shall leave a part of me here. I hear my coach has arrived, and I must hasten . . .

—Francis Thompson, every inch a poet at the beginning of his new life

The Hound of Heaven

I fled Him, down the nights and down the days;
I fled Him, down the arches of the years;
I fled Him, down the labyrinthine ways
   Of my own mind; and in the mist of tears
I hid from Him, and under running laughter.
      Up vistaed hopes, I sped;
      And shot, precipitated,
Adown Titanic glooms of chasmèd fears,
   From those strong Feet that followed, followed after
      But with unhurrying chase,
      And unperturbèd pace,
Deliberate speed, majestic instancy,
   They beat—and a Voice beat
   More instant than the Feet—
"All things betray thee, who betrayest Me."

      I pleaded, outlaw-wise,
By many a hearted casement, curtained red,
   Trellised with intertwining charities
(For, though I knew His love Who followed,
      Yet was I sore adread
Lest, having Him, I must have naught beside);
But, if one little casement parted wide,
   The gust of His approach would clash it to.
   Fear wist not to evade as Love wist to pursue.
Across the margent of the world I fled,
   And troubled the gold gateways of the stars,
   Smiting for shelter on their clangèd bars;

Fretted to dulcet jars
And silvern chatter the pale ports o' the moon.
I said to dawn: Be sudden; to eve: Be soon—
  With thy young skyey blossoms heap me over
    From this tremendous Lover!
Float thy vague veil about me, lest He see!
  I tempted all His servitors, but to find
My own betrayal in their constancy,
In faith to Him their fickleness to me,
  Their traitorous trueness, and their loyal deceit.
To all swift things for swiftness did I sue;
  Clung to the whistling mane of every wind.
    But whether they swept, smoothly fleet,
  The long savannahs of the blue;
    Or whether, Thunder-driven,
  They clanged His chariot 'thwart a heaven,
Plashy with flying lightnings round the spurn o' their
feet:—
  Fear wist not to evade as Love wist to pursue.
    Still with unhurrying chase,
    And unperturbèd pace,
  Deliberate speed, majestic instancy,
    Came on the following Feet,
    And a Voice above their beat—
"Naught shelters thee, who wilt not shelter Me."

I sought no more that, after which I strayed
    In face of man or maid;
But still within the little children's eyes
    Seems something, something that replies,
They at least are for me, surely for me!
I turned me to them very wistfully;
But just as their young eyes grew sudden fair
    With dawning answers there,

Their angel plucked them from me by the hair.
"Come then, ye other children, Nature's—share
With me" (said I) "your delicate fellowship;
      Let me greet you lip to lip,
      Let me twine you with caresses,
          Wantoning
      With our Lady-Mother's vagrant tresses,
          Banqueting
      With her in her wind-walled palace,
      Underneath her azured daïs,
      Quaffing, as your taintless way is,
          From a chalice
Lucent-weeping out of the dayspring."
      So it was done:
I in their delicate fellowship was one—
Drew the bolt of Nature's secrecies.
      I knew all the swift importings
      On the wilful face of skies;
      I knew how the clouds arise,
      Spumèd of the wild sea-snortings;
          All that's born or dies
      Rose and drooped with; made them shapers
Of mine own moods, or wailful or divine—
      With them joyed and was bereaven.
      I was heavy with the even,
      When she lit her glimmering tapers
      Round the day's dead sanctities.
      I laughed in the morning's eyes.
I triumphed and I saddened with all weather,
      Heaven and I wept together,
And its sweet tears were salt with mortal mine;
Against the red throb of its sunset-heart
      I laid my own to beat,
      And share commingling heat;

83

But not by that, by that, was eased my human smart.
In vain my tears were wet on Heaven's grey cheek.
For ah! we know not what each other says,
    These things and I; in sound *I* speak—
Their sound is but their stir, they speak by silences,
Nature, poor stepdame, cannot slake my drouth;
    Let her, if she would owe me,
Drop yon blue bosom-veil of sky, and show me
    The breasts o' her tenderness:
Never did any milk of hers once bless
    My thirsting mouth.
    Nigh and nigh draws the chase
    With unperturbèd pace,
Deliberate speed, majestic instancy,
    And past those noisèd Feet
    A Voice comes yet more fleet—
"Lo! naught contents thee, who content'st not Me."

Naked I wait Thy love's uplifted stroke!
My harness piece by piece Thou has hewn from me,
    And smitten me to my knee;
    I am defenseless utterly.
    I slept, methinks, and woke.
And, slowly gazing, find me stripped in sleep.
In the rash lustihead of my young powers,
    I shook the pillaring hours
And pulled my life upon me, grimed with smears,
I stand amid the dust o' the mounded years—
My mangled youth lies dead beneath the heap.
My days have crackled and gone up in smoke,
Have puffed and burst as sun-starts on a stream.
    Yea, faileth now even dream
The dreamer, and the lute the lutanist;
Even the linked fantasies, in whose blossomy twist

I swung the earth a trinket at my wrist,
Are yielding; cords of all too weak account
For earth, with heavy griefs so overplussed.
  Ah! is Thy love indeed
A weed, albeit an amaranthine weed,
Suffering no flowers except its own to mount?
  Ah! must—
  Designer infinite!—
Ah! must Thou char the wood ere Thou canst limn with it?
My freshness spent its wavering shower i' the dust;
And now my heart is as a broken fount,
Wherein tear-drippings stagnate, spilt down ever
  From the dank thoughts that shiver
Upon the sighful branches of my mind.
  Such is; what is to be?
The pulp so bitter, how shall taste the rind?
I dimly guess what Time in mists confounds;
Yet ever and anon a trumpet sounds
From the hid battlements of Eternity;
Those shaken mists a space unsettle, then
Round the half-glimpsed turrets slowly wash again;
  But not ere him who summoneth
  I first have seen, enwound
With glooming robes purpureal, cypress-crowned,
His name I know, and what his trumpet saith.
Whether man's heat or life it be which yields
  Thee harvest, must Thy harvest fields
  Be dunged with rotten death?

  Now of that long pursuit
 Comes on at hand the bruit;
 That Voice is round me like a bursting sea:
  "And is thy earth so marred,
  Shattered in shard on shard?

Lo, all things fly thee, for Thou fliest Me!
        Strange, piteous futile thing,
Wherefore should any set thee love apart?
Seeing none but I makes much of naught" (He said),
"And human love needs human meriting:
        How hast thou merited—
Of all man's clotted clay the dingiest clot?
    Alack, thou knowest not
How little worthy of any love thou art!
Whom wilt thou find to love ignoble thee,
        Save Me, save only Me?
All which I took from thee I did but take,
        Not for thy harms,
But just that thou might'st seek it in My arms.
        All which thy child's mistake
Fancies as lost, I have stored for thee at home:
        Rise, clasp My hand, and come."
        Halts by me that footfall:
        Is my gloom, after all,
    Shade of His hand, outstretched caressingly?
        "Ah, fondest, blindest, weakest,
        I am He Whom thou seekest!
    Thou dravest love from thee, who dravest Me."

Postscript

Francis Thompson indeed lived for more than a year at the monastery in Storrington, Sussex. He had recently been saved from certain death as a homeless man on the London streets by Wilfrid Meynell, the editor of the Catholic magazine *Merry England*. Meynell employed the young poet as a book reviewer, an occupation in which the young Thompson's erudition could be best put to use. When it became evident to Meynell that Thompson had relapsed into opium abuse, he arranged for the poet to stay at the monastery until he conquered his addiction.

Thompson's biographer John Evangelist Walsh writes,

> I should perhaps also record my disappointed attempt to trace a monastery diary connected with Thompson's year at Storrington, particularly by visiting the monastery's mother house at Frigolet, near Avignon, where it was thought it might have been sent. This diary, whose existence is more than probable, could do much to further illumine Thompson's effort, at the quiet Premonstratensien Priory in the Sussex countryside, to lift himself out of the hopeless, drugged decay of his London derelict days. Despite some earnest searching, however, it has not yet come to light, and I must admit a hope that mention of it here may some day lead to its discovery.[5]

I was, of course, very much intrigued by the idea that Thompson had kept a diary of his recuperation at Storrington; in fact, my imagination took flight. In creating an imaginary diary, I interspersed it with both real people and fictional characters. All of the monks at the Priory are imaginary, but it is possible that religious men much like them lived at

Storrington. It is a fact that Wilfrid and Alice Meynell visited Thompson soon after they read his poem "Ode to the Setting Sun". This ode was startling proof to the Meynells that they had indeed saved a genius from death on the London streets.

Prior to his rescue by the Meynells, Francis Thompson had been saved by a London prostitute who found him at his nadir of opium addiction and physical illness. We do not know anything about her except that she nursed Thompson back to health and disappeared when it became apparent that others had discovered Thompson's poetic genius. Another real person in Thompson's life was Mr. John McMaster, a well-known London evangelical who helped Thompson by giving him work and spiritual counsel but who finally gave up on Thompson when he returned to opium. McMaster is remembered to have said that Thompson was his only failure.

As for the young man Timothy who took his life, he is the product of my imagination. On the other hand, Canon Carroll indeed knew Thompson when he was a boy and always kept in contact with him; it was he who informed Thompson that "The Passion of Mary" was published in Meynell's magazine. It is conceivable that if not for Canon Carroll, Thompson may never have learned that his poem was published. There is no proof that Canon Carroll visited Thompson at Storrington, but such an event is plausible.

Had Thompson ever attempted suicide? According to the diary of the poet, author, and diplomat Wilfrid Scawen Blunt (1840–1922), Wilfrid Meynell had told Blunt that Thompson at least once attempted suicide but refrained when in a vision he saw the boy poet Chatterton, whose help came the day after his own (Chatterton's) suicide.

We now come to Thompson's most famous poem, *The Hound of Heaven*. According to biographer John Evangelist

Walsh, the first inspiration for the poem occurred to Thompson in London in 1888. For the sake of drama I postpone that inspiration to the poet's time spent at the Storrington monastery, where I also have Thompson complete the ode, which was published separately in 1890 and then in Thompson's first book, *Poems*, in November 1893. There is no doubt, however, that most of the ode was written at Storrington.

As for depicting Thompson's inner life, I kept to some well-known facts. Thompson loved Shakespeare and read him all his life. Shelley was his favorite poet, and he indeed wrote his famous essay "Shelley", which was published posthumously to great acclaim, at Storrington. As a book reviewer for *Merry England*, Thompson was perhaps one of the most well-read poets of his time; no writer, whether a philosopher, theologian, mystic, or poet, was beyond his scope.

From the start of my study, Francis Thompson's relationship with his parents intrigued me. His mother and father were both converts to Catholicism and were a very pious couple. Both parents had hoped that their son would be a priest. When their son's teachers advised against this, they decided he would make a fine doctor. Thompson, being a dutiful son and a passive one, never informed his parents about his own dream: to be a poet.

Before her death, when Thompson was about eighteen, Mrs. Thompson presented him a copy of De Quincey's *Confessions of an Opium-Eater*, which transformed the poet's life forever. Like De Quincey, who captured his opium-induced experiences in elegant prose, Thompson hoped to capture his own exotic visions in startlingly gorgeous verse. It is probable, although it cannot be proved, that Thompson became a laudanum addict while attending medical school in Manchester.

By all accounts Thompson's father was a good and compassionate man. But father and son entered into a terrible argument that resulted in the young man's departure from his home for London. Biographers are not sure what instigated the argument, but speculation runs that the poet may have been stealing laudanum from his father's office. His father was a homeopathic doctor, and, like most medical practitioners at the time, he would have had laudanum on the premises for medicinal purposes.

The diary concludes with Thompson freed from his dependence upon opium. Unfortunately, the poet never completely conquered his addiction. Repeatedly, he relapsed and was sent to monasteries, where the silence, solitude, and holy ambiance nurtured him back to health. His health was never strong, and Thompson's biographer indicates that his death was likely a combination of tuberculosis and drug abuse. Current scholars speculate that Thompson might have died from opium alone.

Many teachers of Thompson have failed to inform us that he was an addict most of his life. Perhaps they fear this unpleasant truth can distract some from appreciating the man's genius or tempt others to sin. Surely they want their students to emulate his spiritual strength and not his physical weakness. But knowing that he struggled with opium addiction all his life renders him in my eyes more heroic—and more human. Thompson's life says to all of us: No matter how many times we fail, God will never fail us. He knows our frailty and loves us still, pursuing us relentlessly as a lover his beloved.

Important Events in the Life of Francis Thompson

1859 December 18, born in Preston, Lancashire.
1864 Family moves to Ashton-under-Lyne, not far from Manchester.
1870 Enrolls in Saint Cuthbert's College, Ushaw, to prepare for the priesthood.
1877 Departs from Ushaw after superiors advise that he lacks a vocation. He is admitted to Owens College, Manchester, to prepare for a medical career.
1879 For the first time takes opium (laudanum).
1880 Mother dies.
1884 Departs from Owens without a medical degree.
1885 Leaves home after heated argument with his father.
1886 Now on the streets of London as a homeless man.
1887 In February he submits an essay and poetry to *Merry England*; still living on the London streets. In the summer he is befriended by a nameless prostitute.
1888 In the spring he attempts suicide. Soon after, his poem "Passion of Mary" appears in *Merry England*. In May he first meets Wilfrid Meynell, editor of *Merry England*.
1889 To regain his health he stays at a monastery in Storrington, Sussex. Writes "Ode to the Setting Sun" and the Shelley essay and begins *The Hound of Heaven*.
1890 In March he returns to London to work with Wilfrid Meynell.
1892 Relapses into opium addiction. The Meynells send him to a monastery in Pantasaph, Wales.

1893 First book, *Poems*, is published.
1895 Second book, *Sister Songs*, is published.
1897 Third book, *New Poems*, is published.
1901 Thompson begins four-year period as a book reviewer. He reviews more than 250 books.
1905 Health deteriorates after a return to opium. Also suffers from tuberculosis. He lives near monastery at Crawley.
1906 He returns to London to complete a book of prose, which is never carried through.
1907 He dies on November 13. Postmortem reveals extensive tubercular state. The exact cause of death, from drugs or tuberculosis, remains in doubt.

Endnotes

[1] Rev. Terence L. Connolly, ed., *Poems of Francis Thompson* (New York: Century, 1932), p. 300.

[2] John Walsh, *Strange Harp, Strange Symphony* (New York: Hawthorn Books, 1967), p. 76.

[3] Ibid., p. 90.

[4] John Walsh, ed., *The Letters of Francis Thompson* (New York: Hawthorn Books, 1969), p. 192.

[5] Walsh, *Strange Harp*, ix.

Bibliography

Boardman, Brigid M., *Between Heaven and Charing Cross* (New Haven, Conn.: Yale University Press, 1988).

Connolly, Rev. Terence L., *Poems of Francis Thompson* (New York: The Century Co., 1932).

Meynell, Everard, *The Life of Francis Thompson* (London: Burns & Oates, 1913).

Meynell, Viola, *Francis Thompson and Wilfrid Meynell, A Memoir* (New York: E. P. Dutton, 1953).

Walsh, John, *Strange Harp, Strange Symphony* (New York: Hawthorn Books, 1967).

Walsh, John, *The Letters of Francis Thompson* (New York: Hawthorn Books, 1969).